DUNGEON MASTER

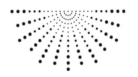

GOLDEN ANGEL

ACKNOWLEDGMENTS

I want to start by thanking everyone who requested a later-in-life kinky romance from me. I loved writing Dungeon Master and I know I'm going to love this whole series so much.

I also need to give a special shoutout to my husband (though he always gets one) and my best friend Katie for helping me through some of the finer nuances of D&D since I had yet to play a full campaign when I wrote this (something that we're currently in the process of changing!).

Another shoutout to my friend Lisa, who is always on-call to answer questions about Pittsburgh for me.

A huge thank you to my alpha readers, Marie, Marta, Karen, Annie, Candida, Nick, and Katherine, and to my beta readers Lesley and Rhonda. All of you helped me make this book so much better than it would have been otherwise.

And thank you to everyone in my Facebook group who immediately jumped in to answer me when I asked about sex after menopause. If the sex scenes came across as relatable and realistic, it is entirely due to the candidness and help of my group!

Lastly - thank you, dear reader, for picking up this book. I hope you enjoyed it. If you did, reviews and/or are always appreciated.

Take care and stay sassy,

Angel

PROLOGUE

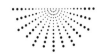

GAVIN

The club was busy, on both floors, as always. Looking around, Gavin felt nothing but pride at what he had built. The Outlands was a safe haven for kinksters, tucked away under what was a bar by day and a popular nightclub for the college students at night. None of them had any idea there was a secret basement full of whips, chains, and an assortment of other toys beneath them while they partied away on the floor above.

His eyes scanned the room. There were plenty of Dungeon Monitors, but Gavin liked to keep an eye on things. The club was set up as one very large room, but when it got crowded, as it did on the weekends, it was impossible to see everything going on. That was the only flaw. If he had to do it all again, he'd design this room with a balcony so he could survey the entire floor from one position.

Control freak.

Maybe a wee bit.

"Master Gavin."

The soft voice made him turn to look down at Brianne, a sweet submissive who had a monumental crush on him. Since she was respectful about it, Gavin tried not to hurt her feelings, but she was becoming more and more forward in her requests.

"Yes, lassie?" He kept his voice short and clipped. Despite his years in the states, he'd managed to maintain his original Scottish burr, but he tried to damp that down now. He knew the submissives thought it was sexy, and he didn't want to encourage her.

"I was wondering if you would like to play tonight, Master Gavin. I would be happy to be of assistance." She peeked up at him, though her head remained down, trying to gauge his reaction to the offer.

Clever girl. She'd chosen a night when his ex-wife, Leah, wasn't here. Despite being divorced, he and Leah scened at Outlands on a fairly regular basis. Their marriage hadn't worked out, but neither of them had been able to get over the other. The bedroom had been the one place they'd always gotten along, and that had continued even after the split.

Gavin never scened with anyone else when Leah was there. He also didn't have sex with any of the submissives he scened with other than Leah, but that didn't seem to stop some of them from hoping. As long as Leah wasn't wearing his collar, he knew this would keep happening.

Raising his gaze away from the young submissive next to him, Gavin didn't feel even a little tempted. Brianne was, what, twenty-five? Less than half his age. It didn't make him feel virile or manly to have young women interested in him. It made him feel *old*. Their hopes and dreams were still intact. They hadn't been beaten down by life yet, whereas he was cynical and jaded.

Except...

His eyes were drawn to the couple across the room—the ones who had come in for the first time yesterday.

Logan had his wife, Felicity, tied to a square wooden column and was flogging her. The two of them had come to Pittsburgh for the weekend, and he liked to keep an eye on any newcomers, but that wasn't the entire reason why his eyes were constantly drawn to them. To be honest, he wasn't sure why. Something about them had tickled his interest.

"Master Gavin?"

The right words, said in the wrong voice.

"Not tonight, lass." Gavin shook his head, turning his attention back to her. "Would you like some help finding another Dom to scene with?"

"No, thank you, Master Gavin." She sighed heavily before walking away.

Gavin's mouth twitched. He wondered if the sigh was supposed to make him feel guilty. If so, she'd underestimated what an ornery bastard he was. It didn't bother him to turn her away.

He looked back at Logan and Felicity. Logan was setting up a Hitachi against the column. Gavin grinned and moved closer. He enjoyed watching a good scene as much as the next man.

"THANKS FOR THE RIDE BACK HOME AND THE HELP," LOGAN SAID AS Gavin parked the car in front of the hotel where Logan and Felicity were staying. The pretty submissive was tucked up next to her husband, lightly snoring. She'd been flying high in subspace after their scene, and Logan had needed some help with her.

"No problem. I didna have anything better to do tonight, anyway." That and he hadn't been able to resist the opportunity to learn more about the couple, even though it meant leaving the club on a busy night. The DMs would have things well in hand, as well as his assistant manager, but it still made him itch to be away on the weekend. "Did you get everything out of the club you wanted?"

He helped Logan slide Felicity out of the backseat. She stirred slightly, moaning a little, but didn't wake.

"We did." Logan grinned, the expression lighting up his face. When Gavin had first met the couple yesterday, Logan had been far more tense, like something was weighing him down. Now he was much lighter. A good scene could do that, but this felt like something more. "I'm sure we'll be back in the future. It's been a long time since we've scened, and it's hard to do at home with the kids around." He shrugged. "We got into a bit of a rut for a while, but we both want to try to stay out of another one."

A rut.

Those were familiar words. Gavin slung one of Felicity's arms over his shoulders while Logan did the same on the other side, allowing them both to support her. He was impressed, Logan didn't seem bothered needing help. Not all men were so secure, but then it was a bit of a way to their room.

"So, this weekend was about reconnecting?" Normally, Gavin wasn't so nosy, but he couldn't help but see the parallels between Logan and Felicity and himself and Leah. Except he and Leah had only had one kid, and they hadn't reconnected. They'd split up instead.

"Sort of." Logan smiled down at his wife, who seemed to have woken up a bit. She was still out of it, but she was moving her feet as they walked her along. "We've been doing the reconnecting thing for weeks now, just working on our relationship. This was more intense, of course, but I don't think it would have gone as well if we hadn't been talking more and spending more time together."

"That was always the part I was bad at," Gavin said, surprising himself with the confession. Logan's words made his chest hurt, stirring up long-dead memories of Leah telling him she was leaving him and trying to explain why. He'd been so young and stupid, so convinced if they'd been 'right,' everything would be easy. It wasn't until he'd gotten older he'd realized how wrong he'd been, but now it was too late... right?

"What?"

"The talking and spending time together," he said, shrugging. They walked through the front door of the hotel, and Logan waved at the man behind the front desk to indicate they were okay. Gavin could only imagine how this looked, but the man waved back. "Sorry, I was thinking aloud."

"Find the right woman, and it becomes easier. We still had to work at it, though."

"Sometimes even finding the right woman doesn't make a difference." Gavin laughed, but it wasn't a happy sound.

Then again, had he really worked at it, the way Logan and Felicity were?

We've been doing the reconnecting thing for weeks now, just working on our relationship.

Gavin hadn't done that. He'd refused to admit there was anything wrong with their relationship. They'd been mostly happy and had plenty of hot sex, so whatever was bothering Leah couldn't be that bad... That's what he'd thought until she'd announced she was leaving him. Looking back, he was able to see how hard she'd tried.

She set up dates for them, which he'd often been late to or had to cancel because of work. She invited him along to all sorts of outings she'd taken with their son, Mitch. Eventually, she asked to go to couple's counseling.

She hadn't made a fuss over the dates, or when he wanted to stay home and relax while she and Mitch were out, or when he'd said no to counseling, so he hadn't realized he'd been driving her away. Not until she finally said she'd had enough and was leaving. Then he'd been ticked she hadn't spoken up for herself before if all those things were so important to her. He'd been convinced he was right, and she was unreasonable. He'd wanted another chance, once he'd known how much it all meant to her, but she hadn't been willing.

I already gave you every chance.

But I didn't know that's what you were doing!

He'd ultimately come to the conclusion while she'd always have his heart, they weren't good in a relationship. Later, he realized *he* might be more of the problem. Yes, Leah should have made it clear when something was important to her, but on the other hand, he could have tried harder. Part of him felt as if he should have known if she was willing to bring something up, it must have been important to her. Leah wasn't one to ask for things, and Gavin had taken that to mean she didn't want anything.

In other words, he'd been a right cunt, and she'd been right to leave him.

Saying goodbye to Logan and Felicity, Gavin wandered back out to his car. The couple was younger than him, but it wasn't too late for them. Maybe it wasn't too late for him and Leah, either.

Something to think about.

CHAPTER ONE

LEAH

"I might be too old for this," Leah muttered, staring at herself in the bathroom mirror. Her blonde didn't show much grey since it had come in silver, and her hair remained light, but she knew it was there.

A first date at fifty-two was nothing like a first date at twenty-three or even thirty-three. At least, she assumed it wasn't. She hadn't had a first date since she was twenty, and she'd been married and pregnant by the time she was twenty-three, but it had to be different, right?

For one, she had never met a man on the internet until now. Get-to-know-you conversations were in person when she'd been dating. Of course, that made her feel even older, as if she should be shaking her fist at her phone and croaking the words 'in my day.'

She didn't have the body she had back then, not that she looked bad now. She liked her body and had always considered herself to be all about self-love and body-positivity, but dating meant putting herself up to be judged by a stranger. It had been a long time since she had to worry about someone else judging her appearance.

Considering how much effort she put into primping, shaving, curling her hair, and putting on makeup—even more than she did when she went to the kink club she regularly attended—her date had better come to the right conclusion. She thought she looked pretty good, but that didn't help the tumble of pre-date nerves in her stomach.

Why am I doing this again?

A plaintive meow had her turning around to see the cute little orange kitten she'd adopted on impulse the other day. She'd gone to the grocery store to get groceries, and there had been an adoption event happening a few storefronts down, and well, one thing led to another.

"Hello, Oliver, who's Mommy's big boy?" she asked, scooping the kitten up in one hand and bringing him in for a cuddle. Purring like a miniature motorcycle on rocket fuel, he rubbed the underside of her chin with the top of his head, loving on her as much as she was on him.

Right. This is why.

Having a newly constant companion had made her realize how lonely she'd become. It was nice to come home to someone who loved her, who cared she was there, instead of an empty house with no life in it. Divorced and with her only son moving out years ago, she'd been the only one in the house until Oliver.

Some people might enjoy the peace and quiet, but Leah didn't. She'd grown up in a noisy household with one big brother and two sisters. The silence of the empty house had been kind of nice for a while, she supposed, but Oliver's presence had fulfilled something she now realized she'd been missing. Suddenly, she'd seen her years stretching on ahead of her, with just her and a cat.

Sure, she could have gone and gotten more cats, but instead, she'd found herself signing up for a dating app. Talking to Oliver was nicer than talking to herself, but having someone who could answer back would be even better. Someone she could spend the rest of her life with, who wanted her for more than sex. She shoved the thought away, determined not to think about her ex tonight.

The door rang, making her jump. Oliver protested when her arms tightened around him a little too quickly, but he was such a good kitty, his protest was purely vocal.

"Sorry, baby," she murmured, hurrying out of the bathroom. She glanced at the clock in the living room on her way to the door. Her date was about fifteen minutes early.

While Leah was all for punctuality, fifteen minutes seemed a little excessive. Should she count that against him? Then again, maybe he'd given himself extra time to find the house and had gotten here early—could be a plus, could be a minus.

"Hi, sorry, I'm…" Her voice trailed off when she yanked the door open, and instead of the in-the-flesh version of OlderGent57, she found herself looking into the piercing blue eyes of her ex-husband, as if that one stray thought had summoned him like the devil he was. Gavin Craig was six feet of confidence and dominance all rolled into one sexy silver fox package that never failed to make her heart turn over.

Her heart *and* the rest of her body. His presence had that much force.

At least he was wearing regular jeans and a shirt instead of his kilt. The kilt was like a weapon of mass distraction. She couldn't think straight when he wore it, and he knew it.

"Hello, love," he said with his usual hint of a Scottish accent and the same wicked grin he greeted her with when they attended Outlands together. The club, which he owned, was one of the two places where they still saw each other regularly, which was another reason she'd decided to start dating again.

She needed to get over the man standing in front of her—the man with a bouquet of Stargazer lilies, her favorite flowers. Leah pretended not to see them. Yeah, dumb, but she was having a miniature freakout, which was perfectly understandable.

"Gavin. What are you doing here?" He *never* came here. This was Leah's sanctuary, the home she'd made for herself after their divorce. There wasn't a single memory of him within these walls, and she *had* to keep it that way for her sanity. Sure, he'd known where she lived, but she never invited him over, and he never came by without an invitation... until now.

Did he have some kind of sixth sense that said, "Leah has a date, go ruin it?"

Instead of answering her question, Gavin locked eyes with Oliver, his brow furrowing.

"When did ye get a cat?"

"Last week." Instinctively, she tightened her hold on Oliver. Gavin wouldn't have made her get rid of a cat when they were married, but he'd always professed himself to not be a 'cat person.' They'd never gotten one, even though Leah had really wanted one. He cocked his head to the side, studying Oliver, who seemed to be studying him just as closely. Dammit. She needed to get Gavin out of here before Simon arrived.

"Gavin, what are you doing here?"

His eyes lifted to meet her gaze, and he gave her a lopsided smile. Not the smile he'd given her before. No, this one was a little less confident, a little more vulnerable, and so much harder to resist. When he spoke again, his Scottish burr was much more pronounced, a subtle declaration his emotions were higher.

"I'm here to win ye back, love."

Her heart thudded into the pit of her stomach as the declaration sent her reeling.

Crap on toast.

***

GAVIN

It was a good thing he hadn't expected Leah to throw herself in his arms in a fit of joy, and he was ready for a challenge, but he hadn't expected the first words out of her mouth.

"I have a date."

Still holding the tiny orange ball of purring fluff against her chest, her expression was more 'deer in headlights' than 'my secret hopes are coming true,' which would have been hell enough on his ego, even without the admission. They'd carried a flame for each other long after they split, and even though she'd been the one to leave him, he'd hoped she'd be a little more amenable to the idea.

Then again, this was out of the blue for her, whereas he'd had months to think about it. To plan. Still, he hadn't expected *that*.

"A date?"

Leah didn't date, not since they'd divorced. Neither of them did. They'd both scened platonically with other partners at Outlands but always kept coming back to each other.

Her chin lifted, and her blue eyes flashed. Gavin looked her up and down. She *was* dressed for a date, but he'd initially assumed ladies' night out or something. Her little black dress hugged every curve—though he couldn't see how low it dipped in the front when she currently had the cat snuggled against her breasts—and her blonde hair was done up in a pretty twist, the kind of makeup that looked so natural it probably had taken twice the amount of time to do than her usual, and high heels that showed off her legs. She was always beautiful to him, but she did look particularly fine this evening.

"Yes, a date, and he's going to be here any minute, so you need to go." She waved her hand at him as if she was trying to shoo him away. She didn't really expect that to work, did she?

"What's his name?" Gavin crossed his arms over his chest, almost hitting himself in the face with the flowers and metaphorically digging in his heels. Leah glared at him. He stared back at her, silently waiting. She knew the fastest way to make him go away was to tell him what he wanted to know.

"Simon Keyserling, a professor of engineering at Pitt. He's fifty-five with no criminal record, and he'll be here in ten minutes. Please go away."

There was a true plea in her voice, but Gavin couldn't go, not yet. Leah going on a date was a wrinkle he hadn't anticipated, but that didn't change his goal.

After meeting Logan and Felicity, he started thinking maybe he could reconnect with Leah. He started reading books about relationships and watching some of the other successful couples at the

Outlands. A couple weeks ago, he visited his son and saw Mitch was starting to follow in his footsteps. Thankfully, Mitch had ended up doing what Gavin hadn't been able to with Leah. He'd made himself vulnerable and got his girl.

It was time for Gavin to do the same. He didn't want to do the half-arsed thing with Leah anymore, taking stolen moments and scenes at the club but otherwise not having anything to do with each other. He wanted laughter and movie nights, arguments and conversation. He wanted to wake up every morning next to the person he loved.

Clearly, she agreed if she was starting to date again. He wasn't opposed to that, but he meant for her to date *him*. Give him another chance and prove they could make their relationship work outside of the club or the bedroom.

"How long have you two been dating?"

Leah rolled her eyes, jiggling nervously. The cat in her arms wriggled, and she relaxed, stroking its tiny head. The little lad was pretty cute, Gavin had to admit, even though he'd never been much interested in cats. He was willing to make an exception for Leah, and she was clearly already attached.

"This is the first date, so I would *really appreciate it* if it didn't begin with my ex standing on my doorstep."

Ah. So, she was going to ignore Gavin's declaration he was there to woo her back. That was fine. He was going to ignore her request to go away because her words incensed him.

"First date? And he's picking you up *here*? Don't you know you're supposed to meet them somewhere, not give out your home address?" He snapped out the words as if they were in the club, not on the doorstep of her house.

"Oh, please, Gavin, we're in our fifties. I hardly think I need to worry about a local professor being some kind of Ted Bundy."

Gavin grit his teeth. This was a side of Leah he'd never quite understood. She was extremely careful about her safety in most regards, but she had some peculiar blind spots. His hand itched to spank her until she understood her safety was *always* paramount, and she was just as appealing at fifty-two as she had been when she was a lass in her twenties. Since they weren't at the club, he didn't have any rights to discipline her the way he longed to. The next time they were there... *If there is a next time.* An uneasy feeling rippled through his stomach.

He'd expected a long road to win Leah back—he hadn't expected competition.

There was a long moment, then the side of her mouth twitched, and her eyes sparkled. Dammit. She was having him on.

"I'm kidding, Gavin. Jax knows him from around campus and signed off on him, and I let Cyana do a full background check on him. It's *fine.* Now, will you please go?"

Little minx, having fun at his expense. Invoking the name of two of their mutual friends did help him relax. Jax was also a professor at Pitt, and Cyana... well, Cyana would do an even deeper dive into someone than Gavin could since she was a private investigator. He'd used her services more than once when researching new club member applications. He would definitely be asking her for the report on this Simon Keyserling.

He wasn't going to go on his merry way. He'd come here for a specific reason, and even though his timing was apparently shite, he wanted to make sure Leah knew he wasn't going to let her go without a fight. That was one of the mistakes he'd previously made and not one he was planning to repeat.

"I'll go. Enjoy your date, but don't forget what I said, love." He grinned at her. "I aim to win ye back." He held out the flowers he'd almost forgotten about during their conversation.

She took them reluctantly, but he saw the flash of appreciation in her eyes. The lilies were her favorite, and he hadn't bought them nearly often enough for her before. Something so small hadn't seemed to matter, but from the books he'd been reading about relationships, the small things often mattered a great deal.

"Thank you for the flowers," she said primly. "But we are not getting back together. That's the whole point of me dating someone *else.*" Despite her prim tone and her glare, she still hugged the flowers to the side where the cat wasn't. The kitty reached out to bat at the cellophane.

Gavin's grin widened as satisfaction laced through him. Yes, she appreciated the flowers. He wasn't nearly as confident as he was pretending, but he did like seeing Leah with her dander up. It meant he still affected her, even if frustrating her wasn't the emotion he'd been aiming to invoke. This wasn't indifference. He could work with that.

"Challenge accepted, *mo chridhe.*"

Leah's eyes widened at the Gaelic endearment he hadn't used since they'd signed the divorce papers. It was something he'd heard his grandfather call his grandmother when he was a child, and he'd used it for her while they were married. Never since.

My heart.

Because she still was. Always had been.

Gavin turned and sauntered back toward his car.

"That was not a challenge, Gavin Craig! Do you hear me? That was *not* a challenge!"

He waved to his ex before getting into his car, leaving her fuming and forewarned. Bet she thought about him on her date. His therapist was going to have a field day when he told her about this, but it was worth it.

CHAPTER TWO

LEAH

That rat bastard. Fuming, Leah refused to lean down and smell the lilies until after he'd driven away and couldn't see her do it. Oliver batted at the cellophane again, seeming to like the crinkly sound. Hmmm. She would have to make sure the flowers were out of his reach. Were lilies poisonous to cats?

Something else to look up.

Dammit, Gavin.

She would have fallen over herself if he'd done this twenty years ago. Hell, even five years ago.

But now? He had to choose *now?* This specific day? Today?

Hmmm.

Maybe he wasn't the only rat.

Putting the flowers down on her kitchen table, her heart still an unsteady thump from Gavin's unexpected appearance, Leah grabbed her phone. Oliver squirmed in her arms, so she put him down on the floor, away from the flowers. Of course, he immediately jumped up onto the kitchen table and started batting at the cellophane again. Well, as long as he wasn't chewing on the flowers.

She kept her eye on him as she called Jax, one of her two friends who knew about her date. There was no way Cyana was the one who had told Gavin—the woman was basically a vault—but Jax... well, he and Gavin were closer, just like she was closer to Jax's wife, Esther. She still hadn't expected Jax to tattle on her.

"Hello? Leah? Are you okay?"

The concern in Jax's voice was enough to soften her, just the tiniest bit. He hadn't seemed worried about her dating Simon when she'd told him, but he was also protective, big old Daddy Dom that he was.

"I'm fine," she said automatically before realizing that wasn't the honest answer. "I mean, Simon hasn't done anything. He's not even here yet. Did you tell Gavin I have a date?"

"What? Gavin? No. Hell, no." Even though she couldn't see him, Leah was sure Jax was shaking his head. Sincerity rang in his voice. "I'm not going to be the one to do that. You're on your own there, sweetheart."

"Okay, sorry, it's just he showed up here a few minutes ago, and I thought..." Her voice trailed off, guilt niggling because she'd been wrong.

"That's okay, sweetheart. I would have thought the same thing," Jax said comfortingly, a touch of amusement entering his voice. "That's one hell of a coincidence. Gavin's timing always was spot on."

"Yeah, for the worst timing ever," she muttered. Jax didn't argue with her. The doorbell rang again, and her heart leapt. "Crap, I think Simon is here." At least, she hoped it was Simon and not Gavin returning for round two.

"Go. Have fun on your date."

She appreciated Jax being supportive of her dating again. It made it easier to hear his encouragement before she went to open the door. Oliver squalled when she took him away from the flowers but was otherwise calm enough. She quickly shoved the bouquet in the fridge, so she wouldn't have to worry about Oliver eating the flowers until after she'd looked up whether they were toxic for him, before hurrying to the front door.

Opening the door with a smile on her face, Leah relaxed when it *was* Simon standing there. Wearing pressed pants and a suit jacket, he was a good-looking man. A silver fox, like Gavin, but a little more salt and pepper than her ex, tall and maybe not quite as well-muscled, but Gavin was in exceptional shape. He also had a little less presence and none of the dominant vibes that hovered around Gavin like a cloak.

That didn't mean he couldn't be what she needed. A lot of men didn't have the same kind of bearing Gavin did, but they were damn fine Doms. She and Simon hadn't *explicitly* discussed sex, but he was aware she was kinky and hadn't seemed concerned. Being with the alpha of alphas hadn't saved her marriage, so maybe what she needed was someone who was less intense. More willing to bend. Someone willing to be vulnerable on occasion.

No matter how she felt about Gavin, that had never been him.

"Hello," she said, smiling brightly. The cheerfulness might have been a little too forced because Simon blinked in surprise. Leah did her best to reel her overenthusiasm back in. Dammit. Gavin had completely thrown her off.

"Hello. Nice to officially meet you, Leah," Simon said, holding out his hand. Leah shook it. It seemed a little formal for a first date, but then she didn't know what she was doing. Maybe Simon felt as awkward as she did. "You are just as beautiful in person as you are in your pictures. Maybe more. And who is this little guy?"

"This is Oliver. I just got him last week." She scratched the kitty under his chin, her smile from the compliment widening further when Simon leaned in and gently rubbed the top of Oliver's head, and the kitten purred. That seemed like a good sign, right? Gavin hadn't done more than stare at Oliver. Not that she should be comparing Gavin and Simon. She needed to get Gavin out of her head—in more ways than one. She gave Simon a brilliant smile.

"Well, shall we?"

***

GAVIN

Leah was dating someone who wasn't him. Of all the outcomes

he'd gone through in his head for this evening, that hadn't been one of them.

He hadn't held much hope for her immediately jumping into his arms, but he'd considered the possibility. She hadn't safe worded, which was how the end of their marriage had begun. If she'd done that, he would have turned and walked away, despite what he wanted.

She hadn't.

Though she had been flustered. Next time, he'd make it clear if she really wanted him to skedaddle, all she had to do was say "Red" and hope it wasn't the first word out of her mouth.

Should he be worried about the date tonight? Pulling into the parking lot of his condo building, he tapped his fingers against the steering wheel. As soon as the car was parked, he pulled out his phone to call Cyana. He would do his own search, but he wanted to see what he could get out of her first.

Tonight had been his opening gambit to see how receptive Leah was. *Not particularly.* That was expected. His goal for the evening had been to get her thinking about the possibility. Let her know he was interested. To show her he had evolved a little.

He had never been very good about bringing her flowers. Perhaps he should get a toy for the cat. That would surprise her.

The ringing stopped, and the phone clicked as Cyana picked up.

"Hello?" As always, her tone was brisk and businesslike, even though she knew who was calling.

"Hello, lass. Tell me everything you have on this Simon." He didn't bother with unnecessary pleasantries because they tended to make Cyana impatient and annoyed. Even so, she sighed.

"How did you even find out?"

"Leah told me." He decided to neglect to tell Cyana the circumstances under which Leah had told him. If Cyana thought it had come up in conversation, she was much more likely to tell him what he wanted to know. "I just want to make sure she's safe. Did you know he's picking her up from her house?"

The frustrated, derogatory noise Cyana made clearly expressed her feelings on the matter.

"Yes. So, I went extra deep. He's had a couple of parking and speeding tickets, none of them within the last three years. Other than that, he's clean as a whistle. No complaints, officially or unofficially, with the police or at the university."

Which meant Cyana had gone digging deeper than the regular reports. That was good. Wasn't it? He didn't want Leah out on a date with a predator. *I don't want her out on a date at all.* Right, but if she was going to be out on a date with someone other than him, better it was a stand-up gentleman. Right?

"Okay, good." He kept his tone as mild as he could.

"You're going to stay out of it, right?" Cyana asked, with only the tiniest bit of threat in her tone. There weren't too many people who were willing to go toe to toe with Gavin, but Cyana topped the list of those who were.

"Out of her and Simon's date? Absolutely." He would absolutely stay out of her date tonight. In fact, he'd been a very good boy and left them to it instead of hanging out on Leah's street, waiting for Simon to show up, then following them to the restaurant. He wasn't that creepy stalker guy, even if he'd considered it for half a second—for her safety, of course.

"Out of her and Simon dating, period," Cyana stressed.

"Sure, lass. I won't bother her and Simon at all." Nope. He was going to be one hundred percent focused on *his* relationship with Leah. If her dates with Simon suffered for it... ah, well, too bad. So sad.

"Be sure you do. Bye, Gavin."

"Thank you, Cy."

Grinning, he turned off his car and headed into the condo building. He'd a setback tonight, but he wasn't out of the game. Not yet. Now he needed to plan his next move, that was all. Maybe he'd pick up another one of those romance books Leah liked so much. They really weren't half bad and gave him plenty of ideas.

LEAH

This wasn't the worst first date in the world, but she doubted it was the best, even though she didn't have much to compare it to. Simon was a nice guy. He clearly loved his job and was interesting to talk to, but there wasn't that massive spark of attraction she got with Gavin.

Argh.

She really wished her ex hadn't shown up right before her date. It would have been so much easier *not* to compare the two men if she wasn't seeing them one right after the other. Not her fault or Simon's, but there it was.

"How's your dinner?" Simon asked, smiling at her.

Leah looked down at her plate. She'd been so engrossed in her own thoughts, she'd barely noticed how the steak tasted.

"Good! It's good. Everything's wonderful. How is yours?" Ugh. Could she be any more ridiculous? Simon probably thought she was a total nitwit.

"Also good." His smile seemed kind. "Is everything alright? You seem a bit distracted."

"Yes... I..." Crud. She owed him some kind of explanation. "I'm sorry. I had an awkward conversation with my ex-husband before you arrived, and it threw me a bit."

"I know how that can be, though I admit, I don't think I've talked to my ex in years."

"Well, we have a son together and have always tried to keep things friendly for his sake, and we have a lot of mutual friends." She pushed her mashed potatoes around on her plate. How much to admit? "We're part of the same gaming group. There are six of us, and we meet up once a week to play games together. We've all been doing it for years... When we split up, we didn't want to wreck that for everyone else, and it seems to have worked out."

This didn't seem like the time for admitting she and Gavin got together several times a year, sometimes more, for kinky hot sex at her ex-husband's BDSM club—if there ever was a time for that. She was allowed to keep some secrets, right? As long as she wasn't *still*

20

doing it with Gavin. And she wasn't and didn't plan to. It had been three months since the last time, and once she made the decision to start dating, she'd told herself no more, not even 'one last time.' Nope, that had been her last time, and she was going to have to live with that. It was better she hadn't tried to make a production out of it.

"What kind of games?"

"Uh, one game." She smiled a little weakly. Even though she knew it was 'cooler' now than it had been when she was younger—some people had actually believed it would lead to devil worship, murders, and crazy things like that—she still felt weird talking about it so openly. It was odd that something she'd once been bullied for playing was now considered 'cool' in some circles. "Castles and Creatures. C&C."

Thankfully Simon didn't seem fazed by her admission about playing one of the 'nerdiest' games out there.

"It's pretty intense. Do you play any games?"

"On occasion. They're not really my forte." He smiled. "When I have free time, I usually prefer to read or be outdoors if I can."

Yes, he'd talked about how much he enjoyed hiking and camping. Leah wasn't against that, although she didn't have a ton of experience with it.

"Oh, yes. I do a lot of reading, too. The game is only once a week, so it doesn't really interfere with the rest of my life. It's just as much an excuse to catch up with my friends." Except it was so much more than that, but if Simon wasn't a gamer, she wasn't sure she'd be able to explain it to him.

"Read anything good lately?"

"Oh, uh…" She wracked her brain. She already knew from talking to Simon, he was a much more intellectual reader than she was. Somehow, she didn't think revealing she was binge-reading her way through the *Black Light* BDSM romance series was going to impress him.

"Is that a bad question for an English professor to ask?" He smiled ruefully. "I didn't mean to put you on the spot."

"No, it's just that I've been on a romance reading kick lately."

Lately, meaning the last thirty years. Which she shouldn't be ashamed of, darn it.

"Ah." He blinked and paused, clearly searching for a suitable response. "Well, I'm sure those are good, too."

"Have you ever read one?" she asked hopefully.

"Ah, well, no. I don't really think I'm their target audience."

"No, probably not." She smiled at him, sighing inwardly. Gavin had never wanted to read them either. She would have loved to read and talk about them with him. He'd read plenty of books with romance *in* them, but he'd balked at reading actual romances. So, she was used to this.

Argh.

There she went, thinking about Gavin again.

Rallying, she managed to get her act together to get through dinner, and by the time they were eating dessert and swapping funny stories about work, she'd relaxed. And when Simon took her home, walking her to the door, and said he'd like to kiss her, she said yes.

It was a very nice first kiss, perfectly serviceable. Nothing at all like the heated kisses Gavin often claimed her mouth with, but it was a *first* kiss. Surely, she and Simon would work up to the passionate kisses.

Surely.

CHAPTER THREE

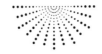

Gavin

Everyone always came to Gavin's for game night since he had an entire room dedicated to Castles and Creatures, which meant they didn't have to move all their pieces every week. Considering how detailed the maps they used were and all the miniatures they had laid out on it, it was for the best. Setting up and cleaning up week after week would have taken a long time, and by the end of the first month, it had been easier to have a dedicated space.

Of course, after he and Leah split, they'd had to move everything, but they'd managed to time the campaign to finish while he was packing up.

It had been two days since he'd stopped by Leah's house before her date, and he hadn't heard from her since. Not that he'd expected to, but he'd wondered if she'd call out sick tonight. All day, he'd waited for her to say something in the group text, but there was nothing.

He'd spent the morning doing the accounting and attending to some other business matters for Outlands, then the afternoon preparing the perfect evening. Everyone always came over for dinner before they started playing, taking that time to catch up and chat as themselves. Usually, it devolved into a discussion of what they wanted to accomplish that evening and trying to get Gavin to give them hints of what was ahead.

He never gave anything away, but he appreciated the effort as well as the opportunity to fuck with them.

Dinner tonight was going to be special. It was his turn to provide, and he'd gone all out, cooking all Leah's favorites. Things he'd made her for special occasions, but rarely outside of them. She'd done most of the cooking, though she'd always insisted it was because she truly enjoyed it. Gavin didn't love cooking, but he could hold his own in the kitchen. Any time he cooked was truly a labor of love, and she knew it.

The front door opened, and Gavin looked up. His condo had an open floor plan, so he could see everyone as they came in the front door unless he was in one of the bedrooms. Unfortunately, it was only Aiden. Gavin raised his eyebrows.

"You're here early."

"Did a run to the hardware store that took longer than I thought it would, and my choices were to go home and be late or come straight here and be early. Holy shit, it smells amazing. Are you... cooking?" The incredulity in his voice was reflected on his face as he crossed the room, following his nose.

A couple inches taller than Gavin, he had dark eyes and hair. Unlike Gavin, his dark hair had remained dark; his goatee was mostly salt with just a bit of pepper still sprinkled throughout. More than one person at the Outlands had compared him to Jeffrey Morgan after Negan had appeared on The Walking Dead. He had the same kind of dangerous air about him, though once someone got to know him, they realized he was more of a mischief-maker than a threat.

"Yes, I'm cooking." Everything had about ten more minutes to go. Cheesy scalloped potatoes with scallions were in the oven, along with lamb stuffed red peppers and bacon-wrapped asparagus. Leah's favorite brand of red wine had been opened and was 'breathing' in anticipation of her arrival, and Gavin had an ice cream cake in the freezer. *That* part he hadn't made—Leah liked Carvel, so that's what Leah was going to get.

"It smells amazing, but what the hell, man?" Aiden's forehead wrinkled as he sat down on one of the bar seats along the opposite side of the kitchen island Gavin was behind.

"Just felt like cooking." Gavin shrugged. He knew Aiden would figure it out pretty quickly, but that didn't mean Gavin had to admit it. All the relationship books he'd been reading said he needed to be more open to communication, but he was pretty sure that was with Leah, not with a friend who was going to tease him about it the first chance he got.

"Uh huh." As expected, Aiden realized something was up. He was observant, which made him a good Dom, but he could also be a pain in the ass. Thankfully, he was also less nosy than some of their other friends and didn't press the issue. "So, what have you been up to lately?"

LEAH

Chill out. This is a totally normal night, the same kind of evening you have every week with your friends and your ex, and there will be absolutely nothing weird about it. There's no way Gavin will make a thing out of your date in front of everyone.

Gavin didn't like letting people see into his personal business because it made him vulnerable. Even when they were splitting up, he'd barely talked to their friends about what was going on. They'd learned most of their information from her.

Nervously wiping her hands on her pants, Leah held her head high and opened the door. On game night, no one knocked since they were expected. The muffled sound of laughter went full blast when the door opened, but it was the incredible *smell* that hit her in the face. That wasn't pizza, Mediterranean, or Chinese food... no...

That scent went straight to the memory bank of her brain, making her tongue tingle and sparking immediate tears as a wave of nostalgia and old emotions slammed into her. *What the actual hell?* It smelled like home and happiness. She was flush with the warmth of knowing Gavin had done something special for her.

The sense of smell is the one most acutely linked with memories.

While she'd known that was true, she didn't think she'd ever experienced it so viscerally.

"Leah? You coming in?" Esther asked, swiveling around on the stool in front of Gavin's counter. "Gavin *cooked.*" The awe and surprise in her voice made Leah's ex laugh, and that sound punched her straight in the gut, thanks to how vulnerable she was already feeling.

"I do know how, you know," he teased. Standing on the other side of the island, his eyes were on Leah rather than Esther. Bright blue watched her every move, cataloguing every reaction. The way he did in the club when she had his full attention as the submissive he was playing with.

When was the last time he'd looked at her like that outside of a scene?

Not since the divorce when he was trying to figure out why she was walking out on him.

I aim to win ye back.

Pressing her lips together, Leah gathered herself back up again. The shock of the memories he'd brought up by cooking some of her favorite foods had fractured her usual defenses, but she was practiced at building her walls against him. She had to be, considering how often they'd scened together after their divorce.

"Sorry, I was so shocked by the smell of home-cooked food, I think my brain tripped." As everyone burst out into laughter, she put a wide smile on her face and closed the door behind her. Everyone laughed except Gavin, who was still watching her with a little smile on his face as if he'd already won something.

Woo-hoo, two points for Gavin—he remembered her favorite flowers and how to cook her favorite foods. Neither of those things made up for... well, everything else. The low bar of expectations she'd had when she was younger was much higher now. She damn well knew she deserved better than what she'd gotten from him before.

She was the last one to arrive, which she'd done deliberately, figuring their friends would provide her with a buffer. Especially since Esther, Jax, and Cyana all knew she'd gone on a date. The only one who didn't know was Aiden. She hadn't meant to leave him out, exactly, but he could be a wild card with his reactions—which was probably why he usually played a rogue character in C&C. He said he wasn't great at improvising, so he preferred to stay true to who he was rather than experimenting.

Leah had pegged him as the most likely to tell Gavin before she was ready, but that was a moot point now.

"You look nice," Gavin said as she approached, and she almost stumbled over her feet.

She'd chosen to wear jeans with a nice blouse and do her makeup and hair—nothing extravagant, just enough to make her feel really good about herself. It was supposed to be armor, not something Gavin noticed, then complimented her on, making her feel all flush and warm inside and even more off-balance. Then again, he was probably aiming to fluster her, so she shouldn't feel too bad if he succeeded a little.

"You do look nice," Cyana said, eyeing her. The Dominatrix was nearly as scary as Gavin. Maybe a little more so at times. Tanned skin paired with dark eyes were set off against dyed silver-grey hair. Once it had started to go grey, she'd decided she was going to embrace the look and dyed it that color instead of the other way around. Although she was the youngest of the group, in her late forties rather than her fifties, she looked even younger despite her hair, thanks to her almost impossibly smooth skin and fit body. As a private investigator, she needed to be in good shape, and she didn't seem to have slowed down at all as the years passed.

"Thanks?" Leah shrugged. "I changed out of my work clothes?" She left both sentences hanging as questions, pretending she didn't understand why they were making a big deal.

Hugs were exchanged, including one with Gavin. He tried to let linger a moment too long, but allowed her to pull away when she stepped back, then handed her a glass of wine. Catching sight of the bottle on the counter, she felt her heart do another little flipping ka-thunk in her chest.

Dammit. Favorite flowers, favorite foods, favorite wine.

Yeah, because he's wooing you. Just remember how quickly this all goes away when he realizes the effort has to be continuous and not every once in a while.

Right. Her chest tightened. She remembered how much it hurt when he'd stopped making these little gestures and started taking her for granted. Again. The smart move would be to enjoy some of her favorite things while not reading anything into them. Once he real-ized she wasn't going to jump back in his arms because he'd put in a bit of effort, he'd give it up. The same way he had before. Only this time, she wasn't going to let it hurt her.

"What are we talking about?" she asked, taking a sip of her wine and inwardly sighing with pleasure as the full-bodied flavor rolled over her tongue, leaving behind a hint of fruit and earth.

"Your son's new girlfriend," Esther said, grinning. She was sitting on one of the barstools with Cyana, while Jax, Aiden, and Gavin had arranged themselves on the opposite side of the island. They looked like something out of a magazine, maybe Esquire. Gavin and Aiden both had full heads of hair. Jax shaved his head to the skin and had a very attractive salt and pepper goatee, fuller than Aiden's rugged scruff but not as expansive as Gavin's beard, and it stood out even more against his dark skin than theirs did. They were all silver foxes in their own right, even if she was only wildly attracted to one of them.

Leah slid onto the last barstool, completing the 'boys vs. girls' setup. She knew the men were being polite and allowing the ladies to sit down, which she appreciated, but it still made her smile.

"Domi, yes." Lovely young woman. She'd come up the weekend before when Mitch came home for Purim, which was one of the Jewish holidays Leah still insisted on him attending for a family cele-bration. They hadn't been a particularly religious family, but Leah liked to celebrate the big holidays, and she knew Gavin liked having Mitch around for Easter and Christmas, even though he'd never admit it. Domi had brought her five-year-old daughter, Ana, which Leah had *loved*. She'd gotten to play grandmother all weekend and was already hoping Domi and Mitch would make it official in the future.

"I was telling them how we finally got the full story on how Mitch and Domi got together," Gavin told her, his blue eyes sparkling warmly as if they were sharing a joke. They were, but he didn't need to make it feel so darn intimate. Darn it.

"And I need to know how it ends," Esther said, leaning onto her elbow and resting her chin on her hand. Half-white and half-Asian, she often joked it was her Korean genes that kept her skin so smooth, but now that she was in her fifties, she was finally starting to get a few wrinkles here and there. They mostly showed up when she smiled. She swept some of her long, dark hair back off of her shoulder. "Gavin's left us hanging. So, they went out to brunch, and she was about to walk out the door..."

Rather than looking at Esther, Gavin kept eye contact with Leah, his blue eyes boring into hers. Despite the buffer their friends were supposed to provide, their presence did absolutely nothing. Something about Gavin had changed. He wasn't pretending nothing was going on between them just because the others were there, the way she'd expected him to, the way he'd always done in the past.

No, he held her gaze, making the moment unnervingly intimate, his lips curling into a little smile as suspicion began to dawn on their friends' expressions.

"Domi was on her way out the door when Mitch climbed up onto the table and declared he loved her."

It wasn't what he said but the way he said it—as if *he* was the one declaring his love at the moment—while he stared straight at Leah.

That's it.

She was going to murder him.

CHAPTER FOUR

GAVIN

The beeping oven timer broke the tension in the room at exactly the right moment, allowing everyone to pretend Gavin hadn't just made things extremely awkward for everyone. Not that he cared. He was uncomfortable, too, but it was worth it. Would be worth it to prove to Leah he'd changed, that he was committed to being a better man, a better partner.

Going to therapy had been uncomfortable, but he'd gotten through it, and Dr. Silverwood had reminded him multiple times being uncomfortable was natural. Normal. Not something to run from. Especially since being vulnerable with his emotions was often uncomfortable but something he would need to do in order to win Leah back. That wasn't her professional opinion about how to win Leah back. That was the conclusion *he'd* come to.

So far, it was working. Leah already didn't know what to make of him being so vocal, neither did their friends, and he'd barely started.

Making sure to get a seat next to Leah, Gavin noticed she stiffened when he sat down, he ignored the suspicious looks everyone else was giving them. Cyana, who sat down across from him, leveled a glare his way. Out of all of their friends, she was the most likely to play guard dog when it came to Leah, but that wasn't going to stop him.

"How was your date with Simon?" he asked, turning to Leah. Aiden choked on the mouthful of lamb he'd just put in his mouth, Jax groaned, Esther froze, and Cyana glared even harder.

"It was fine. I mean good. It was good." Leah didn't meet his eyes, reaching out to grab her wine glass again. "We're going out again this weekend."

Thumping his chest, Aiden finally got himself under control.

"You went on a date?" he asked, sputtering only a little and prompting Cyana, who was sitting next to him, to shoot him a dirty look.

"Don't talk with your mouth full."

"Sorry, sunshine," Aiden said sarcastically but took a long drink of water to help him clear his mouth. Gavin's lips twitched. The two of them were always sniping at each other. It was too bad they were both dominant because they were probably never going to be able to clear the sexual tension constantly simmering between them. Although it didn't stop Aiden from teasing Cyana that she should try submitting to him, whereas she tended to pretend there wasn't any attraction between them.

"Yes, I went on a date. He's a professor at the University of Pittsburgh. Jax signed off on him, and Cyana checked him out." Leah kept her gaze focused on her dinner. Gavin didn't mind. He dug in, grinning inwardly when Leah's elbow accidentally brushed against his when she scooped up some potatoes.

"Right." Aiden's eyes darted back and forth between Gavin and Leah as if looking for cues from them. Gavin smiled at him. Yeah, he was bothered Leah was dating, but he wasn't going to let it slow him down or stop him. Aiden shook his head in confusion and shrugged. "Okay then. So, is the next monster we battle going to be named Simon?"

"Maybe." Gavin winked, and everyone laughed. Even Leah reluctantly giggled. He cast her a sideways glance, but she determinedly ignored him. Hmmm, was this what Aiden felt like with Cyana all the time? That was an amusing thought. Thankfully, the issue between him and Leah had nothing to do with their compatibility.

Being patient wasn't one of his strongest virtues, but he was working on it.

———

LEAH

Studying her character sheet, Leah pursed her lips together.

"If we can stop and rest here, that would be best for me. I can go a little longer, but if we hit any trouble in town..."

"Resting sounds good," Esther agreed. "We *know* this place is safe, but who knows what we're in for once we enter Alderic."

All they knew was it looked well-guarded and had high walls, and it was on their way to the House of Starrett, which was their final destination.

"I'll sleep next to Ysolde," Aiden said, wiggling his eyebrows at Cyana. "In case she gets cold." Cyana rolled her eyes, though it was impossible to tell if she was doing it in character or as herself. Aiden's character took every opportunity to flirt with Cyana in a way he could never do as himself. It had become a long-running joke of their campaigns that eventually, Aiden's characters would fall in love with Cyana's, and it didn't matter how grotesque she'd made some of them.

"You wish, Morag."

"I really do." He winked at her roguishly.

"I think this would also be a good time to take a real break," Esther said, her voice altering to her real register from the slightly higher voice she used when she was being Leandrin Longleaf. "I need to refill my drink."

"I could use a bathroom break," Leah agreed, stretching. She felt Gavin's eyes on her and quickly pulled her arms in. Did he think she'd been stretching to get his attention? She totally hadn't—she didn't hate how it got his attention, but she *shouldn't* want his attention.

Dammit. He had her completely confused.

She hadn't asked for this—wouldn't have asked for it—but she couldn't deny some little part of her was enjoying it. Even though she wasn't going to give in.

Gavin sat at the head of the table, slightly separated from everyone by both space and the DM screen propped up between him and them. During their breaks, Aiden often tried to get a peek at it when Gavin wasn't there. He didn't actually want to know, but he knew it drove Gavin up the wall.

Normally, that meant Gavin spent most of his time hovering near his side of the table, even when they were on a break, to keep Aiden away. Which was why the very last thing Leah expected was to reach the closed bathroom door in his hallway and out of the corner of her eye, see him walking toward her. Her head whipped up, turning to face him, eyes widening with surprise, hand still on the doorknob.

"What are you doing?" She didn't know why she whispered, it just happened naturally.

"Maybe I need to go to the bathroom." He stepped closer, getting into her personal space, looming the way he did in the club. The way he had at home when they were still married. Leah's heartbeat stuttered, her breathing becoming shallow as her pulse began to race. Stupid physical reactions she couldn't control.

Back away! Move!

That was the smart voice in her brain, the one dedicated to emotional self-preservation. Unfortunately, her body didn't seem to be listening. Her head tipped back to look up at him, and she was brutally aware of how close they were standing. Was he going to kiss her?

Do I want him to?

"Gavin," Cyana barked, and Leah jumped, her head snapping toward the sound. Standing at the end of the hallway, Cyana was scowling at Gavin, hands on her hips. "A word?"

Straightening, Gavin winked at Leah, then sauntered down the hallway to Cyana, leaving Leah feeling shaky and... disappointed. A part of her had wanted to kiss him.

I'm in so much trouble.

GAVIN

Dragging him out onto the balcony where Aiden and Jax were waiting, Cyana crossed her arms over her chest as soon as she got him out there. The night was warm, with the slightly chilly breeze that happened in early spring. The looks all three of his friends were giving him were chilly as well.

"What the hell are you doing?" Hands on her hips, Cyana glared at him, her dark eyes sparking with protectiveness and irritation. "You cannot play games with Leah like this!"

"Who says I'm playing a game?" He raised his eyebrows. Might as well come clean now that their dander was up. Gavin had hoped for a little more time to work on Leah before having to admit what was going on to their friends, but he hadn't expected Simon, so he'd been a bit bolder than he'd initially anticipated. "I realized I wanted Leah back before I knew she was going on a date with Simon."

Cyana's eyes narrowed, and she started to open her mouth to say something, but Gavin cut her off.

"You can ask Mitch." He'd already told his son his plans. Mitch had been wary, but he hadn't discouraged Gavin once he'd been told everything. "Or my therapist."

Cyana's mouth snapped shut. Both Jax and Aiden stared at him.

"*You're* seeing a therapist?" Jax asked, his deep voice full of disbelief. Gavin knew Jax didn't think he was lying, but it was such a surprising statement, he was having trouble believing it—and he clearly wasn't the only one.

"For the past few months."

Enjoying their reactions, Gavin leaned against the balcony, shoving his hands in his pockets. They were the precursor to how *Leah* would react. Seeing what an impact it had on them made him hopeful she would also be moved. Hell, after their little interlude in the hallway, he was feeling buoyant. If Cyana hadn't come along, he was pretty sure Leah would have let him kiss her.

"You want Leah back? Like back, back? Not the 'we have sex at the club and pretend it means nothing' thing you two have been doing for years now?" Aiden's skepticism didn't exactly pop Gavin's balloon of hope, but it did remind him what a hard road he had ahead of him. That was good. He shouldn't forget it was going to take a lot of work to get Leah and himself to where he wanted to be.

"Aye." He nodded his head, shoving his hands in his pockets.

"What does Leah think about this?" Cyana asked, crossing her arms over her chest and giving him a hard look.

Gavin shrugged.

"What did it look like to you?" He raised his eyebrow. A thoughtful expression crossed her face. *Ha.* He had her there. "I think she wants someone in her life, and I mean for it to be me. Not Simon. Or anyone else. And she needs someone. She's already adopted one cat."

"One cat is starting her down the road to crazy cat lady?" Jax asked, his lips twitching with amusement at Gavin's hyperbole.

"It could be, but I don't mean to let it get that far."

"You dumbasses." Cyana scowled at all three of them, causing Aiden to hold up his hands in immediate surrender. "You think choosing to have a cat instead of a man is somehow a bad thing for *her*? If Leah wants a cat instead of you, that has nothing to do with her and everything to do with *you*."

Something uncomfortable shifted inside Gavin's chest. Yeah, he knew the cat lady thing was a stereotype, but there were often truths backing up some stereotypes. Right? Yet the way Cyana phrased it felt like she was insulting *him*.

"You can't tell me you'd rather have a cat than a man," Aiden said, looking at her incredulously and—thankfully—taking the heat for Gavin.

"Welcome to the twenty-first century, fellas." Cyana rolled her eyes, enough sarcasm lacing her voice to bite. "Women are now allowed to own property, apply for our own credit, and have careers, which means we have the money to buy our own houses and cars. We have the internet, online shopping, and a whole great big world of sex toys to fulfill our needs. 'Crazy cat ladies' are just women who have done the math and realized a vibrator and a furry animal who shits in a box can fulfill their needs just as well, if not better, than a man. If you can't appeal more to her than a cat, that's a personal problem on your end—not hers."

Giving Aiden a pointed look, she spun on her heel and went back into the condo. Through the glass, Gavin could see Leah had returned from the bathroom and joined Esther on the couch.

"Well, shit," Aiden said, watching Cyana stalk back into the room and sit with the other two. "Do you think she's telling on you right now? Should we intervene?"

Giving the matter some consideration, Gavin shook his head after a moment.

"She might be annoyed over the cat thing, but I don't think she'll say anything about that to Leah. She won't want to hurt Leah's feelings. And I don't care if she tells Leah I'm seeing a therapist." Leah was going to find out eventually since Gavin planned on asking her to go with him. Turn the tables on the requests she'd made of him in the past. Right now, Leah could probably use some time with her two best friends. He turned back to his. "Let's give them a minute."

Leah

Shutting the sliding door behind her, Cyana stalked inside and sat in one of the armchairs across from where Leah and Esther were on the couch. She moved with almost lethal grace, even when she was dressed in her regular clothes outside of the club.

"What are they talking about out there?" Leah asked, pretending she wasn't a bundle of nerves. Esther knew something was going on, but she hadn't probed—yet—probably been waiting for Cyana, hoping she would take the lead. It was harder to deflect with Cyana.

"What do you think?" Cyana asked, raising her eyebrows at Leah. "Were you going to let him kiss you?"

Esther gasped as heat filled Leah's cheeks. Yeah, this was why she and Esther waited for Cyana when they wanted to interrogate each other. She got the job done a lot faster than either of them would.

"Gavin was going to kiss you?" Esther whispered, leaning in, her eyes darting to the glass partition between them and the men. "Like *kiss* kiss you? Outside of the club?"

Sighing, Leah scrubbed her hand over her face, then winced when she remembered she was wearing makeup because she wanted to look nice. Hopefully, she hadn't just smeared mascara everywhere.

"He says he wants to get back together. To win me back." Two different things, one with infinitely more meaning to her than the other. Had he realized that? Or did they mean the same thing to him? She rubbed the spot on her forehead right between her eyebrows, avoiding her eye makeup. "I think he might even mean it."

"Oh, I definitely think he does. Apparently, he already told your son his intentions," Cyana said. Esther let out a soft gasp at the same time as Leah.

Gavin told *Mitch*? Why hadn't Mitch warned her? Her poor son. He'd hated it every time she and Gavin went through their usual cycle, had never understood it, and Leah had never had quite the right words to explain it.

What had Gavin said to him to make it okay? Dammit. Now she wanted to call Mitch and interrogate *him*. Cyana was watching her carefully, gauging Leah's reactions, reading who knows what into her body language. Considering Leah didn't even know how she felt about all of this, she couldn't help but wonder what conclusions Cyana was coming to.

"We need a ladies' night," Esther muttered, eyeing the men outside. They were all straightening up as if they were getting ready to come back in. "This weekend?"

"I have my second date with Simon on Saturday," Leah said. Her stomach did an unhappy little flip. She wasn't dreading it, but she just wasn't looking forward to it the way she thought she should. Relationships took time to grow, so she shouldn't read too much into that. Right?

"Friday night?"

"I'm free," Cyana said.

Leah nodded just as the men came back inside. She avoided

Gavin's gaze, feeling a blush start to fill her cheeks again. He'd told all their best friends he wanted her back and talked to their son. She didn't know how to react to that. The Gavin she remembered would have never done that because he wouldn't have wanted everyone to know if she rejected him.

Who was this man who was putting his pride on the line for her, and what the hell was she supposed to do with him?

CHAPTER FIVE

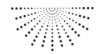

LEAH

"What did your father say to you about us?"

"And hello to you, too, Mom." Mitch's voice was filled with amusement. "So nice to hear from you. I'm doing well, thank you."

She suppressed the smile threatening to form on her lips. Mitch got that sassy sense of humor from her, but she was trying to be serious. She probably should have at least said hello when he answered the phone, but she was a bit pressed for time. Instead of waiting to call him during the evening, she'd called during the workday in between meetings because she hadn't been able to take her curiosity any longer—she needed to know.

It was unlike her to be so demanding, but she only had a few minutes. She really should have waited till the end of the day to call. Somehow her patience had flown right out the window along with her usual reticence for being so rudely direct. Still, she took a deep breath because she knew Mitch was right. She'd not only bypassed gracefulness, she'd completely skipped over her manners.

"Hi, honey. I'm sorry, but I only have a few minutes to talk, and I recently discovered you and your father had a conversation about me and him?"

There was a short silence. Leah jiggled her foot under her desk, tamping down the urge to throttle her only offspring through the phone. It wasn't as if it was the first time she'd had that urge. She loved her son with every fiber of her being, but sometimes, he was just as frustrating as his father, and that was saying something.

"Yeah, Dad mentioned he was interested in trying to rekindle things with you." There was a hint of caution in his voice as if he wasn't sure how she would take that revelation.

"Uh huh, and did he say anything else?"

Another silence.

"I think maybe you should talk to Dad about this."

"Really?" Leah scowled. "After all the years of butting your nose in and asking why your dad and I can't stay apart, *now* you're choosing to keep silent?"

Her son chuckled, then sighed.

"Let's just say, while he was down here, I learned some things about you and Dad, I wish I hadn't. He also said some things that make me think he's learned a few things he should have a long time ago."

Well, crap. Gavin had gone down to D.C., where Mitch lived, to visit another kink club and talk with the owner about the way he'd expanded his business. Leah could only imagine what Mitch might think about that. Yup. Did not want to know. Especially since she'd already had a sneaking suspicion about Mitch and his girlfriend, Domi, after their recent visit. Like parents, like son, it appeared. Ugh, she did not want to think too hard about that.

"I'm sorry," she said, not sure what she was apologizing for, but it felt like there must be something.

"Don't be sorry, just be careful," Mitch replied, quoting back to her one of her favorite sayings from his high school years. Leah laughed, relaxing slightly. She loved her baby boy so much, no matter how old he got, and had hated feeling his judgment over the years every time she and Gavin had... hooked up? Spent time together? Briefly reconciled? All of that felt far too casual to describe their on-again, off-again sexual relationship.

"Does this mean I'm not going to have to listen to a lecture from you if your father *does* convince me to try again?" Only half-joking, she was curious how Mitch felt since he'd always been so vehemently against his parents reconciling in the past—in any way, shape, or form.

Another long moment of silence and Leah's eyebrows started climbing toward her hairline. She'd expected a sigh or some kind of quip from Mitch, not this thoughtful quiet.

"I know it sounds weird, but I think he might have really changed. Did you know he's been going to therapy?"

Heat swept through her, followed by cold; not physically, but that's what it felt like. Anger was quickly frozen out because she couldn't afford to rage in the middle of her office during a workday when she had a meeting in a few minutes.

Old anger and resentment because she'd *asked* Gavin to go to couples' therapy with her. It had been so hard to work up the courage to do so, and he'd shot her down. Hadn't thought they needed it. Of course, he'd offered it up as a last-ditch option when she told him she was leaving him, but by then, it was too late, and he certainly hadn't gone on his own.

Until now.

"He is?" Her tone was stilted, full of old pain, old bitterness.

"Yeah." Mitch was quiet again for a long moment while Leah did her best to sort out her feelings. She had no idea what to say. "If you want to give him another chance, I'll stay out of it. I want you to be happy, Mom. That's all I've ever wanted."

"I know, sweetheart."

There was a knock on her door, and she looked up as Brandy, the number two on her marketing team, opened it and peeked in. Leah raised a finger to indicate she'd be there in one minute.

"I have to go. I have a meeting. Give Domi and Ana my love."

"I will. Say hi to Dad for me."

Her son's blithe acceptance she would not only see Gavin some-time soon but giving her a message to pass on to him shook Leah almost as much as the revelation about Gavin going to therapy.

Somehow, Gavin had their son quietly rooting for them or at least no longer rooting against them.

She didn't have time to think about that right now. Shaking her head, she gathered up the files in front of her. She couldn't wait for ladies' night with Cyana and Esther. They were as unbiased as she could get, and she needed to talk through everything with them.

Gavin remained on her mind for the rest of the day, and she couldn't quite shake him loose.

* * *

GAVIN

The hard knocking on his door was unexpected, and Gavin frowned as he headed to answer it. He wasn't expecting anyone, and when he glanced through the peephole, he was even more flummoxed. What was Leah doing here? Shit, if he'd known she was coming by, he would have put on a shirt.

On the other hand... He glanced down at the grey sweatpants hanging low on his hips, his bare upper body, and the sprinkling of hair across his chest. It wasn't like she hadn't seen his chest before, but they hadn't scened in a couple of months. Maybe he shouldn't discount the whole 'answer the door shirtless after a shower' thing. Remind her of what she was missing out on while she was dating Professor Simon.

Pulling open the door, he cocked his head as he looked down at his ex-wife.

"Gav—" Her voice cut off as her eyes widened, getting caught on his chest before working their way down.

Gavin grinned.

Flexed.

Unfortunately, the flexing was too much, distracting Leah, so she brought her eyes straight back up to meet his, flustered but already hard at work to gather herself back together.

"We need to talk." Head held high, she pushed past him, her shoulder brushing against his chest, though she pretended not to notice. Gavin rubbed his skin. The light touch had tickled his chest hairs.

"Well, hello to you, too," he said, closing the door behind her, only a bit of sarcasm in his voice. "Come on in."

Leah came to a halt, turning around to look at him, an odd expression on her face. Nothing to do with him being shirtless, he was fairly sure, but he couldn't quite interpret it.

"What?"

"Nothing. Just... Mitch said something similar to me earlier today. I thought he got that bit of sass from me, but now I think maybe it's you." She shook her head, her lips twisting to a sad smile.

"Maybe it's both of us." He'd noted a lot of similarities between himself and Mitch of late as well. More than he'd ever realized. He hadn't told Leah that Mitch was a member of a kink club down in D.C. He wasn't sure Mitch would want her to know and was fairly certain she wouldn't want Mitch knowing about them. Too late on the latter, but at least he could keep her in the dark about their son's sex life.

"What can I do for you, Leah?"

He prowled closer, and her eyes darted down to his chest before coming up to meet his gaze. Putting up a hand in front of herself, as if to ward him off, she didn't step back. Gavin came close enough, her hand hovered in front of his skin, close enough to brush against his chest hair. Her pupils dilated, and her quick intake of breath proved she wasn't immune to him, no matter that she'd decided to start dating other people.

"I..." She dropped her hand as if burned, tucking it behind her back. A frown crossed her face, then cleared, and she lifted her chin up defiantly. "I wanted to talk. It seems as if you've been talking to a lot of people except me. Our son. Our friends. A therapist." She raised her eyebrow at him.

Gavin wondered whether it was their son or their friends who had told her about the shrink. He was guessing Mitch since she was confronting him this morning instead of last night after the game.

Last night, she'd darted out the door with Cyana rather than allowing Gavin to walk her out to her car.

"Dr. Silverwood." Gavin leaned in closer, lowering his head a little —just as he had last night before Cyana had interrupted them. "Would you like to come with me to my next appointment?"

Unfortunately, he hadn't anticipated Leah's reaction. Her eyes widened, and she stepped back, taking her out of reach of his lips, though not his hands. The impulse to reach out and touch her remained, but he let her retreat. If this was going to work, she needed to *want* to come to him.

Crossing her arms over her chest, she glared at him.

"Just like that? I asked you to go years ago, and you said no."

"And then I said yes."

"Not until you knew I was leaving, and you only said it to get me to stay."

"Yes, because I didn't want you to go."

"If you didn't want me to leave, you should have said yes when I asked you to go!" Her voice was getting higher, louder, her cheeks turning pinker with frustration and anger.

Taking a deep breath, Gavin made himself relax. His fingers tingled, partly from wanting to clench his fists and partly from wanting to turn her over his knee. Leah stared at him with wounded, frustrated eyes. He'd seen that expression on her face all too often at the end of their marriage, felt this way all too often, but that was then, and this was now.

He wanted to break the cycle, which meant he had to be calmer. Think about what he wanted long-term, not short-term. Yes, he was still frustrated over what he'd seen as Leah's lack of communication, but he could see it from her perspective. She had asked, even if she hadn't told him how important it was to her. If he'd known she was thinking about leaving him, he would have gone. Probably. He liked to think he would have. But she hadn't told him why she wanted to go, and he'd thought she was following a trend or something. He hadn't known how important it was to her until it was too late.

DUNGEON MASTER

He didn't remind her of that. Instead, he took a second deep breath and nodded his head.

"You're right. I should have." There was a certain amount of pain connected to saying the words, yet also relief from acknowledging his own wrongdoing. "I should have known you wouldn't have asked to go on a whim. And while I wish you had been more forthcoming about your reasons for asking, I also wish I'd probed deeper instead of assuming everything was fine because I was fine."

That knocked the wind right out of her sails. Leah stared at him, her mouth slightly agape, not knowing what to make of his response. It sure as hell wasn't something he'd have said in the past. Dr. Silverwood would be proud of him.

"I'd like it if you came with me to an appointment. I told her I hoped you would sometime soon. She specializes in couples, but she also sees individuals who want to work on relationships. She's been seeing me for the past few months."

LEAH

The slightly crooked grin on Gavin's face was almost boyish. It was rueful, hopeful, and disarming, all in one. And she didn't know how to handle it.

Coming here had been a mistake.

She should have realized it the moment Gavin opened the door, and the sight of his naked, tattooed, and completely sexy chest overwhelmed her field of vision. Unfortunately, her hormones had kicked into overdrive, and her brain had stuck with her original plan rather than aborting the mission until a better time. It wasn't that she was that horny all the time, but it had been a couple months since they'd scened, and her fickle libido had decided it was *on* today.

So, she'd tried to start a fight, even though she'd come here to talk to him, calmly and rationally, about his recent declaration and interest in therapy. Instead, she'd lashed out. Picked at an old wound.

For a second, it had been working. Then he'd turned the tables on her.

Apologized.

Took responsibility.

And made her an offer.

It's a trap.

Yes, thank you, Admiral Akbar.

What if it's a good trap with candy at the end?

"It's okay if you're not ready yet." Gavin rocked back on his heels. The expression on his face was placid, but his eyes were intensely focused on her. He wasn't nearly as blasé as he was pretending. "I go every week, so whenever you want to come, you'll be welcome."

"You've been going to see a therapist every week for how long?"

"About six months now."

The answer flummoxed her. Cocking his head to the side, Gavin took a step closer again, not looming but closing the distance, invading her space to test if she'd back away again.

She didn't.

She should.

But she didn't

This is a bad idea.

Her breath caught in her throat as a little light in Gavin's eyes flickered when she stayed where she was. The space between them closed even farther.

"Leah?" Gavin's voice deepened, saying her name like a caress. His head dipped until their faces were only a few inches apart. It felt like every part of her body came alive, sensitive and aware of how closely they were standing. They weren't quite touching, but they might as well have been. Blue eyes bore into hers, studying her intently.

They had scened at the club after their divorce, but even there, they'd avoided certain things, anything that felt too intimate. Like this. In moments like this, the rest of the world might as well not exist.

"Yes?" Her voice was high. Breathy. She barely recognized it.

I'm old enough to be wiser than this.

That voice was feeble in comparison to the pulse pounding in her ears and the arousal spreading along her limbs to her core.

"I'm going to kiss you now."

Leah tilted her head back, closing her eyes as she waited for his lips to descend to hers.

47

CHAPTER SIX

GAVIN

Brushing his lips over Leah's in the gentlest, most fleeting kiss he'd ever given her, Gavin placed his hands on her hips, pulling her in against him.

"Tell me yes, Leah." Their lips were still touching, just barely, so she would be able to feel his moving against hers when he made the request. Her eyes were still closed, her breath warm against his face when she sighed. "Tell me you want me to kiss you."

"Yes, Gavin, kiss me." She whispered the words as if she didn't dare say them any louder and break the spell they were under.

It did feel like a spell—a stolen moment in time, where there was no one else in the world and no consequences to think about.

Gavin claimed her lips. He was hard as a rock, his cock digging into the softness of her stomach. At his age, that wasn't always a guarantee, especially without some warmup, but just having Leah here, under his hands, asking for his kiss... Fuck. At the club, their contract was spelled out nice and neat. They both knew the boundaries, and they knew it didn't leave the Outlands.

This... this was messy. Dangerous. This was more than sex or getting their needs met.

Kissing for the sake of kissing...

He backed her up to the wall, one step at a time. Felt her gasp when he pressed her against it, trapping her between him and the hard surface. His hips rocked forward, rubbing his cock against her front, and she moaned. Her hands moved over his skin, sliding up to his chest where her fingers rubbed through his chest hair.

When was the last time they'd kissed like this? He couldn't remember. It wasn't that they didn't kiss at the Outlands, but they didn't spend any time on it, didn't let it mean anything.

This... this meant something. He didn't know what yet, but he knew this wasn't emotionless. Leah wouldn't be kissing him like this if she didn't feel something more than attraction.

Rolling his hips, Gavin pulled his lips away from hers, dropping kisses along her jaw, then moving to her neck. Leah gasped, her hands resting on his shoulders and gripping as she wriggled against him. He slid his hands up her sides to her breasts, cupping the soft mounds.

Her back arched, and she moaned his name.

Fuck.

Gavin's cock throbbed as he felt her legs part. She leaned all her weight against the wall, letting him touch her how he pleased. It would be so easy to strip her down and take her right there...

Except she wasn't ready yet. They weren't ready yet. Sex had always been the easy part for them. Too easy sometimes. Like right now. He was getting carried away with wanting her, but they hadn't settled anything yet. And she had a date this weekend.

Growling under his breath, Gavin made himself end the caress and ease away. Leah leaned against the wall, staring at him, eyes wide and hazy with lust. Her chest lifted and fell as she panted, just as hot and ready to go as he was. Gavin mentally cursed the necessity of pulling away. That's not what this was about.

"What's wrong?" she asked, a flicker of hurt crossing her face.

"I didn't mean to take this so far," he admitted, holding up his hand to stop her from responding. He gestured at the front of his sweatpants, which hid absolutely nothing. "I want you, but this isn't all I want. I want more than a sexual relationship with you, Leah. I want everything."

Too soon. It was too soon, and he knew it the moment he saw the panic on her face.

"I have to go."

"Okay." He stepped back. It took every ounce of willpower he possessed. Fuck, he wanted to hold her in his arms and beg her to stay. She needed time. Gavin hadn't listened before when she'd told him what she wanted—needed—from him, but this time he was going to do better, which meant shoving down his own impulses and waiting for her to know what she wanted.

"Think about what I said about coming to a therapy appointment with me. You're welcome any time."

Avoiding his eyes, Leah just nodded and rushed out the door, leaving him standing there with a hard-on from hell, hoping he hadn't just cocked everything up.

LEAH

"He wants you to come to therapy with him?" Esther asked as if she was trying to figure out some hidden meaning behind the words.

"Yes."

"And he *didn't* try to have sex with you?" That was the part Cyana was still hung up on.

To be fair, Leah was a little hung up on it as well. Two days later and her body was still humming with a need her vibrator hadn't been able to handle. It wasn't that her vibrator couldn't get her off, but that wasn't everything she wanted. She wanted the weight of a man on top of her, the feel of his hands moving over her skin, the taste of him in her mouth...

Yup, her libido—rarely reliable—had woken up with a vengeance and didn't appear to be going anywhere. Figured. At her age, she sometimes didn't feel the need for sex for days, even weeks, but now that she shouldn't have it, her body had decided it was all in.

50

"Say it a little louder, why don't you?" Esther hissed, looking around to see if any of the nearby tables were staring at them. They'd decided to start their evening out at a nice restaurant before heading back to Cyana's. Looking nice, feeling nice, then chilling out together and getting drunk, but Esther was already well on her way to the last part since she didn't drink much anymore. Cheeks already a little flushed after two glasses of wine, even a little tipsy, there were certain things she never wanted to talk about in public.

Leah's lips twitched with amusement. You could take the Baby Girl out of the club, but she was still a Baby Girl. Not that Esther and Jax came to Outlands all that much anymore, but they still stopped by occasionally.

"There're no kids around," Cyana said, waving her hand. "If the adults can't handle a little conversation about sex, they don't have to listen."

"He said he wants more from me than a sexual relationship." Leah was doing her best to get the conversation back on track. Of course, she managed to say that at the exact moment their server appeared at their table with their dinners. Now Esther wasn't the only one blushing—only Cyana was unbothered. Cheeks flaming red, Leah couldn't meet the young man's eyes as he put her plate down in front of her.

"Shrimp and grits, chicken cordon bleu, and the New York strip steak, medium rare," he said, setting them down one at a time. Esther's cheeks were a hot red, and she avoided looking at him as well —and when her gaze met Leah's, she blushed even more furiously. "Anything else I can get for you ladies?"

Was she imaging it, or did his voice have a little flirtation in it?

"We'll let you know," Cyana said, smiling up at him. Of course, *she* wasn't fazed at all. "Thank you."

"Absolutely."

Leah peeked up at him in time to see him wink at Cyana, who winked back. As soon as he was out of earshot, Leah leaned forward. Cyana was still watching him walk away.

"He is half your age!"

"Which means he's in his twenties and needs someone to teach him a few things," Cyana said with a grin, finally looking away and turning her attention to the steak in front of her. "But fine. Let's get back to talking about you and Gavin not having sex."

"Oh my God, Cyana." Esther scrunched in her seat, covering her face with her hands. "Can't we talk about the therapy now and the sex later? After I've had a few more drinks, and we're not in public?"

"Fine," Cyana sighed, then made a happy humming noise when she took her first bite of steak. Leah knew how she felt. The shrimp and grits were perfectly cooked, practically melting on her tongue. Damn, she'd needed this. "Are you going to go to therapy with him?"

"Do you think I should?" Leah had to admit she was tempted. Seriously... Gavin in therapy? It felt like something she should witness firsthand. On the other hand, she still had a lot of resentment built up from when she'd been the one trying to get him to go with her. "I mean, he had his chance, years ago, and didn't want it then. Why should I jump just because he finally decided to get on board?"

"I guess it depends on what you want," Cyana said thoughtfully. "If you want a second chance at a relationship with him—a real one, not the act-that-shall-not-be-named-in-public thing you've been doing for the past few years." Esther scowled at her, but Cyana ignored it and kept going. "Then you might have to accept he was just very, very, *very* slow on the uptake."

"Better late than never?" Esther quipped. They all laughed, but Leah still felt unsettled.

"Is it, though?" she asked, making the other two laugh again. She was only half-joking. They were right. The real question... was it *too* late?

GAVIN

The Outlands was hopping, as it always was on a Friday night. Leather and lace, sex and seduction, the sounds of pain and pleasure all intermingling. Unfortunately, he couldn't enjoy it the way he normally did, when all he could think about was Leah and grit his teeth in frustration that she wasn't here. He hadn't been expecting her, but now that he knew she was dating, he wasn't as confident about the nights she didn't come in.

Tomorrow, when she was actually out on a date, was going to be pure torture. Maybe he shouldn't have put his hands on her last night. If he hadn't kissed her, he wouldn't be feeling this hopeful. For once, he wished his appointment with Dr. Silverwood was sooner rather than later. He wasn't seeing her until next Wednesday, but he could use someone to talk everything out with.

"Hey. Hey. Hey. Anyone home? Helloooooo in there?" Aiden waved his hand in front of Gavin's face.

Yeah, unfortunately, he was stuck with Aiden as a confidant for now.

Sighing, he turned to face his friend, raising his eyebrow.

"Do ye need something, laddie?"

"Och, aye," Aiden responded in the worst Scottish accent Gavin had ever heard. He had to suppress his smile. Yeah, his brogue had come through pretty thick, thanks to his roiling emotions. Thankfully, Aiden dropped the terrible accent. "What's going on? You look like you're barely paying attention to the scenes, and that never happens."

Gavin's first instinct was to say nothing, but that wasn't true, and he knew it wasn't helpful. He'd seen Leah's reaction when he'd shared some of his feelings in front of their friends. Seemed like it was something he was going to need to get more used to.

"I can't stop thinking about Leah."

To his surprise, Aiden recoiled, making the sign of the cross in front of himself as if he was trying to ward off evil. The horrified expression on his face was so exaggerated, it was comical.

"Wait, seriously? You're supposed to say, 'I'm fine.' Man up, man. I am not the right person for this." Despite his reaction, and even though he was shaking his head, Aiden showed no signs of fleeing. He was a good friend, even if he was an ass.

"You're the only one who's here, and you asked."

"Yeah, but you're not supposed to give a real answer. Suppress that shit, man. Bury it deep. You're fine. I'm fine. We're all fine." Aiden gestured to the club at large. "Everybody is fine. That was supposed to snap you out of it, not open up a conversation."

"You know you sound like a poster boy for toxic masculinity, right? Do you think it's possible this worldview has anything to do with the fact you've been divorced twice?" Tilting his head at Aiden, Gavin raised his eyebrows, genuinely amused.

Aiden only took a moment to think about the question. "Nah."

Snorting, Gavin couldn't help but chuckle. His friend was a git sometimes, but he was entertaining. Dressed in his leathers and a vest, Gavin was surprised Aiden wasn't out there, finding a likely submissive to scene with. When was the last time he'd seen Aiden actually do a scene? He frowned.

"Are *you* okay?"

"Me? Yeah, of course, I'm fine." Aiden grinned. The lighting where they were standing, off to the sides of the actual scenes, was dim, so Gavin couldn't tell if Aiden was completely serious or not.

"You haven't scened in a while."

Aiden turned away, so Gavin was looking at his profile while Aiden looked out across the club, one of his shoulders lifting in a shrug.

"Does it ever get kind of boring to you?" For Aiden, that was being vulnerable, and Gavin's concern ratcheted up a notch.

"Boring?"

"Yeah, it's the same thing, over and over again. Sub wants this, sub wants that. Spank this one, flog that one. To keep it interesting, I find myself doing things I'm not actually interested in, just to do something different." Aiden shrugged again, shoving his hands in his pockets in an almost defensive gesture.

Unfortunately, Gavin couldn't really relate. When he scened with Leah, he was always so focused on her and her pleasure, on seeing how she reacted to various things, he didn't get bored. But then, they had a connection beyond the sexual encounter for the evening, even when they'd tried to make their relationship all about sex.

"Have you thought about trying for a longer contract with a submissive instead of scening for one night, then dropping her?" Gavin asked, keeping his tone mild.

"Yeah, but then they start expecting things, and I have to be the jerk who lets them down." Aiden sighed, and there was more to it than letting out his breath. It sounded heavy, tired. "Since we're being all touchy-feely, I feel old and jaded, man. I find myself coming here more to see my friends than to get my freak on. And that's weird."

Something suddenly occurred to Gavin.

"Is this why you've been flirting more with Cyana? Are you looking to switch?"

"What? Hell, no!" Aiden jerked back, appearing to be horrified again. "I mean, yeah, I'd love to scene with her, but you know... with me in charge. I feel like that's the kind of challenge that could kick me out of my rut."

"That's the kind of challenge that could get your nuts cut off." Gavin shook his head. There was no freaking way. If he had to lay down money on Aiden vs. Cyana, he'd back Cyana every time. Aiden, well, he wasn't exactly a lazy Dom, but he'd gotten lazier as he got older. Perhaps because he was jaded or cynical, but maybe his heart wasn't really in it anymore. "Do you want to take up with some of the new trainees? Maybe helping them figure out their limits will help you."

"Maybe." Aiden made a face, but he hadn't said no. "It can't hurt to try something new, right?"

"That's pretty much my philosophy right now."

Leah

Sprawled on Cyana's couch, which was very comfortable, Leah was pretty sure she would never be able to move again. The cushions had sunk in, and she was trapped. She would just have to live here forever.

The good news was living on Cyana's couch would probably mean she wouldn't have to face Gavin again... unless they moved game night to Cyana's house, but as long as she was stuck on the couch, there would only be so much Gavin could do to her.

"What's that noise?" she asked. Something was beeping.

"I think it's the oven," Esther said from the other side of the couch, struggling to her feet—and so far, she was losing the struggle. This was why Leah wasn't even trying.

"Stupid needy oven," Cyana muttered under her breath, getting up and heading into the kitchen. How did she do that? Then again, it *was* her couch. She was probably used to having to battle it for supremacy.

Despite being stuffed full at the restaurant, especially after dessert, once they got to Cyana's place and started really drinking, they had the munchies. Thankfully, Cyana had tater tots in her freezer, but Leah was going to have to sit up to eat them.

She pushed and heaved, managing to get herself into a sitting position. Woo-hoo! The couch was still winning the war, but she'd take the battle and be happy for it. Sighing, she glanced over at Esther, who was still struggling to sit up.

"Here, take my hand." Leah held her hand out. Esther reached. Strained. Their fingers touched, and she pulled Esther upright.

"You two are pathetic," Cyana said, chuckling as she came back into the room with a plate full of tater tots piled high.

"I can live with that, as long as there's ranch." Esther grinned, bouncing with excitement now that she was upright. Cyana shot her a look.

"Of course, there's ranch. This is a respectable household. Now eat up. We need the grease to counteract the hangovers in the morning."

Ugh. Yeah, she wasn't wrong. Leah was not looking forward to that part, but she was also having too much fun to really care at the moment. *Worth it.* At least, she thought so now. She might change her mind tomorrow.

"I think I might need to sleep over," Esther muttered.

"Will Daddy let you?" Leah teased. Jax was pure Daddy Dom, and

Leah couldn't remember a time he'd ever let Esther do a sleepover unless it had been pre-arranged. He liked having her home.

"I'm not sure he'll care."

The bitterness in Esther's voice took both Leah and Cyana by surprise, and they exchanged a glance. Crap, was that the alcohol talking? Or was the buzz letting her be more honest than she might have been otherwise? Leah hadn't noticed anything amiss between Jax and Esther, but would she have? As if she'd realized she was bringing the mood down, Esther smiled as she reached forward to take a tater tot off the stack.

"Don't mind me, ladies. Jax has been working late a lot and hasn't had as much time for me, and I'm annoyed."

"Want the name of a couples' counselor? I hear Gavin has a good one," Cyana said, a light note of teasing in her voice, but her concern was clear.

"We'll see." Esther sighed, chewing thoughtfully. "Mmmm, this is exactly what I needed. I think I'm probably too sensitive. I hate being home alone in the evenings."

"What about the kids?"

"They're teenagers." Esther shook her head. "I'm the last person they want to hang out with."

Ah, yes, Leah remembered those years. Mitch had been pretty good about spending time with her; she'd often thought it was his way of trying to prevent her from spending time with Gavin. Look how that had turned out. A decade later and her ex was finally ready for couples counseling. Ugh.

It was too late, right? Surely, it was too late. Too much water under the bridge. Too many old resentments. Too much history and hurt.

But what if...

CHAPTER SEVEN

GAVIN

Should he knock?

No. She might not want to see him this morning.

If he didn't, she might not realize she had anything outside her door.

Plastic bag full of Leah's favorite hangover cures hanging from his hand, Gavin shifted, staring at her door. Was it presumptuous or thoughtful to think she might have a hangover this morning? He didn't remember a ladies' night ending without one while they were married.

He wasn't used to second-guessing himself like this. Maybe because he wasn't used to trying to anticipate what Leah *might* need instead of fulfilling those she *asked* for.

He hadn't done a great job of the latter by the end of their marriage. Dr. Silverwood said it wasn't all his fault, communication did take two people, but the guilt about how much he'd taken Leah for granted didn't go away easily. He also didn't want to let himself off the hook because he knew he could have asked her more often. Should have. And he should have listened when she *did* finally ask him for something.

Rubbing his hand over his chest where it felt particularly tight, he stared at her door.

Only to hear a car pulling up behind him. Turning, he realized Leah hadn't even been home as she pulled into the driveway. Large, dark sunglasses covered her eyes, and her hair was done up in a bun. The sunglasses were big enough, they obscured most of her expression, making it impossible to tell what she was thinking, but he was ninety-nine percent sure she was staring at him.

Of course, she's staring at you. You're standing in front of her house, ya cunt.

Getting out of the car, she kept staring at him. He wished he could tell what she was thinking, but it was impossible while she was wearing those massive sunglasses.

"Gavin?" Her voice was a little rough, a little croaky, and sent him right back to when they were in their thirties, and the first time she swore she was never drinking again. Hangovers hit harder after twenty-five, but it had been their thirties when she'd mostly stopped getting drunk, even when things were at their shittiest.

"I brought you some orange juice." He lifted up the bag. "And a sausage pretzel."

Even with the glasses on, he could see the way her face lit up. The pretzels were damn good. He made them himself after discovering them at an Amish market when visiting Mitch down in Maryland. Sadly, there weren't any close enough to Pittsburgh to get them on a regular basis, so he'd ended up recreating them as best he could. He'd always made them for Leah as hangover food. Another one of his food gestures of love.

Leah picked up her pace, hurrying over to take his offering. As she got closer, he could see the tightness around her lips and the way her forehead was creased, as if she had a headache.

"Seriously? Thank you. You didn't have to do this." She hesitated after taking the bag, thinking about inviting him in.

It was better if he stayed away... for now. She had a date tonight.

"I know, but I wanted to. I know how you lasses get." He grinned down at her. A little smile lifted her lips. He couldn't see her eyes, but he took that as a win.

"We had fun. How was your night with Aiden and Jax?"

"It was the Outlands. Same old, same old. No Jax. Aiden and I hung out most of the night. I'm going to put him to work with some of the trainees."

"That sounds good." The smile had slipped from her face, and she was frowning. "No Jax... maybe I misunderstood Esther. I thought he was going to the Outlands."

"Haven't seen him there in weeks. He and Esther don't come in much anymore. Was he supposed to be with us last night?" Crap. Was there trouble in paradise? Esther and Jax were the couple who seemed to have it all together. Two kids, a happy marriage, and they'd made it far longer than Gavin and Leah had, though they'd gotten married a little later, too. Their youngest was about the same age as Mitch had been when Gavin and Leah divorced.

"I guess not." Leah sighed. "Esther said he's been working a lot lately. She wasn't real happy about it."

Great. Something else for him to worry about. Strangely, he couldn't stop smiling despite now being a little concerned about Jax and Esther. He and Leah hadn't small talked in a while. When they were alone together, it was all about the scene they were about to do, or they talked about Mitch. They sure as hell didn't stand around chatting.

Progress. That's what this was.

But she had a date tonight. He should leave now while things were on a good note. Let her keep this in her head when she was out with Simon later.

"Hopefully, it's a short-lived thing. You should get inside before your pretzel gets cold." Leaning down, he brushed a kiss over her cheek, noting her quick intake of breath as he did so. "I'll talk to you later. Have a good evening."

By 'have a good evening,' he really meant, 'I hope you spend tonight thinking about me and not your date.' Damn, it was going to suck waiting to hear how her second date with Professor Simon went.

LEAH

Dammit, Gavin.

He'd ruined her second date with Simon just as thoroughly as he'd ruined her first. Maybe more. Even hours later, all she could think about was how he'd shown up with her favorite morning-after-drinking food, which he'd made himself, and they weren't exactly effortless. Oliver had tried to steal a bite, and she'd had to resist giving in to his pathetic mewing. She didn't want to teach him bad habits.

Plus... she didn't share sausage rolls.

Hmmm, no matter how bad their marriage had become, Gavin had always made them for her after a night of drinking. Somehow, she'd forgotten that. She'd never had to ask. He'd just made them. It had been one of the things she'd really missed after they split. Making them herself wasn't the same, especially since she was usually cranky and had a pounding headache when she tried.

So, now she was out at dinner with Simon, and all she could think about was Gavin's sausage. Which would be funny later, but right now, she was too frustrated to laugh about it.

"Leah? Is everything okay?" Jerked out of her thoughts by Simon's direct question, Leah shook her head, trying to shake off her distraction.

"Yeah, sorry, Gav— I mean, Simon! Oh my God, I'm so sorry." Horrified, Leah felt something turn over in the pit of her stomach. There was no way she could possibly be more mortified than she was at this moment. "Um, everything's great. The food is great. I'm just a little distracted. I'm so sorry."

At least you didn't call him Gavin's name while you were having sex.

Seriously? That was the best she could do for an upside? They weren't anywhere near having sex—the way things were going, she

61

didn't think they were going to be. Not that she was super interested in having sex with Simon. He was attractive, and a nice guy, and had a certain aura about him, but the chemistry between them was lacking.

Besides, she couldn't help comparing—literally—everything about him to Gavin. And now she'd gone and called him by her ex's name, so there was no pretending about *what* was distracting her.

Simon sighed, a rueful smile on his lips, but there was hurt in his dark eyes. It made Leah feel even worse. She'd almost feel better if he was a jerk about her slip-up. Cyana and Esther were going to give her hell when they heard she'd called him by Gavin's name.

Crap. She couldn't tell them. What if they told Gavin? Or if Esther told Jax, who then told Gavin?

Oh my God, stop thinking about Gavin and start focusing on this date before it turns into even more of a train wreck.

Somehow, she managed to get through the rest of the evening without losing focus again. It still wasn't a good date, not by any standard, and it got worse when Simon walked her to her door at the end of the night.

He was generous, incredibly kind, attractive, funny, understanding, and it killed her she couldn't be more interested in him. Here was this amazing guy who liked her, and instead of falling head over heels for him, she was still hung up on the ex and the crappy relationship she'd left behind a decade ago.

Be fair—you've still been fucking him for most of that decade, so it's not like it was totally over.

Yeah, that didn't make it any better.

When they reached her door, Simon smiled down at her, similar to the smile he'd had in the restaurant. Leah inwardly sighed, already knowing it was over.

"Leah, I really like you. You're funny, you're smart, and I really enjoyed getting to know you." Simon's tone was sympathetic, but it didn't matter.

Leah still wanted to sink into the ground and never come out. *Should have just let Cyana's couch have its way with me.* She was totally getting dumped, and deservedly so.

"But I think it's probably best if this is our last date."

"I'm so sorry," she said, rubbing her hand over her face. She felt lower than dirt. And stupid. She felt monumentally stupid. If this was someone else's life, she'd be screaming at them to go with Simon and leave Gavin behind for good. Unfortunately, that was apparently much easier said than done. "You're a great guy, and I... I'm a hot mess. My ex told me he wants me back, and it's turned me into a total mess, and you deserve so much better than how I'm treating you."

Simon chuckled, his expression lightening a little. "Actually, it's almost nice to hear it's because he's made a move. I'd hate to feel like I lost a competition to a specter from the past."

"Not a specter at all, unfortunately. I am so sorry. Again. I probably should have canceled tonight, but I still wanted to try..." Her voice trailed off miserably.

"I'm glad we tried."

Simon kissed her cheek and left. Even *that* kiss wasn't as good as the one Gavin had given her that morning.

Dammit. Gavin so owed her after this, and since it was a Saturday night, she knew exactly where to find him. Scowling, she decided against going inside and went straight to her car. She didn't want Oliver to think she was home only to abandon him again, and she had a certain meddling man to confront.

GAVIN

The Outlands on a Saturday should have been a good distraction, but Gavin couldn't think about anything but Leah.

Scene with wax play?

Remembering the last time he and Leah had used wax. *Which was fun. Should try that again sometime. If she lets me.*

Scene with cock and ball torture?

Reminded him of his own frustrated libido. Sure, the male submissive Cyana had tied up to the St. Andrew's cross was having a much rougher time than Gavin was, but he was also enjoying it on some level. Gavin had nothing but frustration and no guarantee it would come to any fruition.

Scene with two men and one woman?

Made him think about Professor Simon and Leah—not that he wanted to share her—but since she was currently seeing another man, that was where his head went.

"Master Gavin?" Veronica, one of the club's long-time submissives, came rushing up to him, worry all over her face. Not much threw Veronica off her game, so for the first time all night, his focus narrowed to a single point. "Eben's having some trouble with Master Don."

Crap. Eben could be a bit temperamental, but she was a good switch and rarely had any real trouble with anyone. He knew that guy had been a mistake. Don had talked a good game, but Gavin had a feeling about him during the member interview. Gavin would happily toss him out on his ass if he deserved it.

"What's going on?" he asked, striding after Veronica as she led him toward the other side of the Dungeon. There were so many people, he couldn't see every scening space. "Where are the Dungeon Monitors?"

"He touched Eben's hair. Mistress Terrin is there, but he's not listening to her."

Stupid wanker. Touching Eben's hair was a hard limit for her, and there was no way she would have scened with anyone who hadn't gone over her list. And he wasn't listening to Mistress Terrin? Gavin started moving faster.

Gavin pushed through the small crowd already forming around one of the stations. Terrin and Don were facing off, with her standing between him and Eben, while one of Don's buddies—Michael—was standing behind the man, uselessly wringing his hands. Two other submissives were standing on either side of Eben, who looked as if she was about to launch herself around Terrin and go after Don herself.

Terrin and Don's voices were already rising as they argued.

"You aren't in charge—"

"Do you not understand what 'Dungeon Monitor' means?"

"I don't have to listen to you!"

"Actually, you do." Gavin stepped up beside Terrin, crossing his arms over his chest and glaring at Don. "Listening to the Dungeon Monitors is part of the agreement you signed when you joined."

Huffing, Don tilted his chin up. A little older than Gavin but not in as good of shape, he had thinning blond hair and an almost permanent sulky expression. His friend, Michael, was a little shorter, a little thinner, with grey hair and a wife at home who he had only brought to the club once. It wasn't Gavin's business, but he had the sneaking suspicion Michael's wife had no idea *he* was still coming to the Outlands. Unlike Don, who always wore leathers, Michael tended to show up in suits as if he was coming from work.

"She's not listening to *me*," Don complained, putting his hands on his hips and glaring at Terrin. "This is all a stupid mistake, and she completely overreacted."

"Uh huh. Why don't you tell me what happened then?" Gavin would give the man enough rope to hang himself. That or dig himself out of the hole he was already in, but Gavin was willing to bet the former was more likely.

"We were scening, and I had just tied Eben up and wanted her to tilt her head back, and I grabbed her hair. I forgot it was a hard limit, okay? It's a weird one, and it was an honest mistake. I wasn't thinking. Then this bit— uh..." Don's smooth words faltered when Gavin and Terrin glared at him. He was smart enough to catch himself. "Then *she* came along—"

"Because Eben used her safe word, and this jackass didn't stop." Terrin spat the words out, and Gavin didn't have to look at her to know her eyes were blazing with fire.

"I was going to! You didn't give me a chance." It sounded more like whining than a real protest.

The crowd around them murmured disapprovingly. Drawn by the spectacle, more Dungeon Monitors were converging. Gavin had a feeling he was going to need them to drag Don out. He didn't seem the type to go willingly. The shit gibbon didn't even seem to think he'd done anything wrong.

"You told me to stop being so dramatic," Eben yelled from behind Gavin. There were a few small noises, and he didn't turn around, but he'd bet her two friends were keeping her behind Terrin and Gavin. It wasn't as if Eben couldn't protect herself—she could do it a little too well. Something Don didn't seem to realize. "When a submissive safe words, you're supposed to fucking *stop,* asshole!"

"See? She's disrespectful and insulting. Neither of these *women* was willing to listen." Don's lip curled up in a sneer. He was the worst kind of Dom—a misogynist on a power trip masquerading as a Dom. Not a real Dom at all. Sadly, it was something that happened all too often. The good news was, this was Gavin's club, and he didn't have to put up with these wankers in his club.

"*You* should have been the one listening. Eben is completely correct. You should have stopped the moment she said her safe word. Period. You do not call the submissive overdramatic. You do not try to continue the scene. And you listen to the Dungeon Monitors." Gavin shook his head as Don's expression grew more mulish. Fuck it. "Actually, you don't need to worry about any of that because I'm revoking your membership. You ignored a submissive's safe word and a Dungeon Monitor. You're out of here."

"Hey! You can't do that!" Don's face turned bright red, his fists clenching at his side. If he was stupid enough to get physical, he was going to be in for a big surprise. He'd be *lucky* if Gavin was the one to deal with him rather than Terrin or Eben.

Michael finally stepped forward. Not to try to get Don under control or talk him out of being an ass, of course, but to defend him.

"It's not that big a deal. Can't you give him another chance?" Michael asked, worriedly glancing at Don.

Seriously? Ignoring a safeword wasn't that big a deal? Ignoring a Dungeon Monitor?

"And now both of your memberships are revoked." Gavin raised his voice a little louder. "Anyone else who thinks ignoring a safeword isn't a big deal can also take a hike."

"Wait!" Michael was completely shocked. Idiot. No wonder he and Don were friends, although Michael now stepped away from Don as if he was trying to put some distance between them in the face of the consequences. "I didn't even do anything. You can't kick me out. *I didn't break any rules!*"

"What's Rule Zero, everyone?" Gavin asked, keeping his voice loud enough to carry. He stared straight at Don and Michael.

Everyone within hearing distance spoke in a kind of kinky Greek chorus.

"The Dungeon Master makes the rules."

Damn straight. And he was the Dungeon Master.

Gavin's smile was hard-edged as he took a step forward, gesturing to two of the other Dungeon Monitors who were waiting for his signal.

"David, Gareth, escort these men out." He focused back on Don and Michael again. "Your membership fees will be refunded. Do not attempt to come back. And if you break the nondisclosure agreements you signed, I am sure Mistress Terrin here will have a ball suing the hell out of you."

"Hell, I'll do it for free." Terrin grinned like a shark. Michael and Don paled, finally seeming to give up in the face of everyone arrayed against them. Murmurs of disapproval followed them as they were escorted out the door, and Gavin let out a long sigh.

As he was turning back to see how Eben was doing, he came to a halt when his eyes met the gaze of the last person he'd expected to see here tonight, and he froze. Leah stared back at him. Was she here to help make his night better or worse?

Honestly, he could see it going either way.

CHAPTER EIGHT

LEAH

Watching Gavin take out the trash was always hot as hell. That was one of the things Leah had always loved most about him—he'd wanted to create a safe space for people to be kinky together, and he'd done it. Sure, the two asshats who had just been escorted out of the building probably wouldn't agree it was a safe space for *them*, but that's because they were the ones who'd been making it unsafe. People like that never saw themselves clearly, evidenced by the fact they were still muttering about how unfair it was as they were escorted out of the club.

She didn't pay them too much attention.

Nope. Her attention was all for the hot Scot, silver fox, Dungeon Master who had totally ruined her first attempt at dating someone other than him. The big jerk.

She watched as he talked to Eben and Mistress Terrin before nodding and letting them go on their way. Poor Eben looked peeved. She and Terrin walked off, heads together, probably discussing how to torment some poor submissives. After so many years of being at the Outlands, Leah could tell when Eben was feeling subbie and when she was feeling more dominant. She might have started out the evening submissive, but that's not where her headspace was at right now.

Leah could almost understand that since she'd come here, prepared to take Gavin down a peg or two. She'd felt all "I am woman, hear me roar." Watching him kick out the two dingbats, something inside her had shifted, and now that he was actually headed her way with an intense look on his face and heat in his eyes...

Well, her subbie side was not only prevailing, it was squashing practically everything else.

It had been too long since she'd been in the Outlands. The scenes going on around them, the smell of leather and sex, the laughter, cries of pleasure and pain, and soft murmurs of intimacy... felt like a fantasy, but it also felt like home. Being here made her body ache— she expected certain things to happen to her when she was here.

And by certain things, she meant orgasms.

Great. My pussy thinks it's Pavlov's dog.

Come to the Outlands, get wet.

Things had been a little more unpredictable when she was going through menopause, but now? *Wouldn't need any lube tonight.* Considering the circumstances, she wasn't sure that was a benefit.

Gavin came to a halt in front of her, and a fluttering sensation pulsed through her body as she tipped her head back to look at him. He raised his eyebrows.

"Interesting club wear."

Jerk. She scowled.

"I'm still dressed for my date... which *you* ruined. Sir." She clenched her fists by her sides to keep from poking him in the chest, the way she would have done outside the club. Maybe confronting him in an area where he was master of the domain wasn't the best idea, but patience and restraint had completely deserted her.

"How did I ruin it? I wasn't even there," he protested, but he was grinning.

"You know what you've been doing." Her voice was getting higher, and some of the people who had gathered to watch the debacle with Don were turning to look at her and Gavin. Leah felt a blush heat her face, but she didn't care. They could think whatever they wanted. She'd reached her limit. Rather than holding back, she poked him in the chest, hard enough he reached up to rub the spot, surprise clear on his face.

"I got dumped tonight! On the second date! By a perfectly nice man who I had a lot in common with!"

She poked him again, right above where his hand was, and this time he caught her wrist, his expression darkening.

"Ye need to watch yourself there, lassie," he growled. Frowned. "Or is that what you're going for? Topping from the bottom, are ye?"

"What? No."

Yes. Dammit. A part of her was hoping he would take control of her. She was feeling wildly out of whack, horny as hell, and frustrated beyond belief. A scene, some pain, and an orgasm were *exactly* what she needed right now.

Gavin pulled her forward by the wrist he was holding. His other arm wrapped around her, fingers gripping her long, loose hair at the base of her skull and pulling her head back, so she was forced to look up at him. Heat and need rolled through her like a wave as she was pressed up against him, throat bared to him.

Someone in the crowd watching them sighed with envy, and Leah couldn't blame them.

This was fucking hot.

GAVIN

For a few minutes, he'd really thought the night was about to get even worse, but then she'd challenged him. Pushed him. She'd known exactly what she was doing. Leah had been his submissive for too long to think she could get away with that kind of behavior in the club. She was topping from the bottom, though she should know by now, it never worked quite the way she hoped. It didn't matter. She bratted and pushed, and he went to top her. That was how it had always been between them.

The moment he pulled her in, she melted against him, submissive, eager, and waiting. His cock jerked to life for the first time all evening. Bloody hell, he wanted her—even if she was trying to manipulate him.

On the other hand, if he really had ruined her second date and got her dumped... Well, he should take advantage of that, shouldn't he? If she was having sex with Gavin, she wasn't going to feel comfortable finding another boyfriend. She hadn't during all the years they'd been scening together.

Yes, he wanted more than a physical relationship with her, but this could tie into it.

Hell, maybe they could both get what they wanted. Dr. Silverwood likely wouldn't approve, but it wasn't her decision.

"Come with me to therapy this upcoming Wednesday, and I'll give you what you need tonight," he murmured, keeping his voice low, so no one else would be able to hear him. The music and other sounds in the club easily drowned out softer conversations, making the offer completely private, despite the number of people watching.

Leah's eyes flashed.

"Seriously?" She wriggled against him, trying to pull away, and Gavin shifted his hands. The one holding her hair moved to her neck, getting a firmer grip, and the other twisted her arm up behind her back, pressing her fully against him from knees to chest. Leah whimpered, and he rocked his hips forward, rubbing his cock against her soft stomach.

"Seriously. Do we have a bargain, love?"

Her pupils dilated, her breath coming in soft short pants. Bloody hell. Leah was more turned on than he could have believed. He should have done this weeks ago.

"Fine." She bit off the word. "I'll go see your therapist with you on Wednesday. Sir."

"Good." He grinned, his hold on her tightening. "Let's seal it with a kiss."

Bending his head, he claimed her mouth, her lips parting beneath his with a moan, her entire body softening against him. Submitting to him. Fuck he'd missed this. Missed her. The time between their scenes was always too long, and he had a feeling she hadn't meant to scene with him again once she started dating someone else. Leah wasn't the type to go on a date with a man one night and sleep with a second on another.

The best way he could keep her from dating anyone else was to get her back into bed with him on a regular basis and keep her there. He was pretty sure that wasn't just his dick's logic.

Now he just had to figure out what he was going to do with her tonight.

Lifting his head up, still holding her tightly against him as if she might bolt, he did a quick scan of the room to see what stations were open. *Ah... perfect.*

<hr>

LEAH

Weak-kneed, conflicted, and totally turned on, the urge to lean against Gavin's chest and let him take over completely was more overwhelming than usual. It was something she'd struggled against every time they'd scened ever since their divorce. In the back of her head, she knew he couldn't be relied on. He wouldn't be there the next day—hell, he wouldn't even be there when she went home that evening.

It's just physical. That had been her mantra for years now. It was all she'd wanted from him—all she'd allowed herself to want.

Now, it was like there was a decade's worth of pent-up need swelling behind her normal defenses, trying to get out and throw itself at Gavin's feet, begging him to take over. Claim her submission and make her truly fly, the way he'd used to when they were married, and she still thought they had forever ahead of them.

Leah didn't even know if she was capable of that. She'd been so much younger, trust had been easier, and cynicism hadn't taken over. Physically, things could still be amazing. Since menopause, she'd had the enjoyable side effect of being multi-orgasmic under the right circumstances, something Gavin had found delightful, but that wasn't the same as truly submitting—giving herself completely over to him, with all her trust, and sliding into a headspace where she truly wouldn't have any control.

"This way, love." He cradled the back of her neck in his large hand, making her feel submissive and feminine as he led her through the club. Part of her thought she should protest being called 'love,' another part figured she should just be relieved she wasn't his *mo chridhe*, and the last part of her was thrilled at the endearment and simultaneously disappointed he wasn't using Gaelic.

The clashing desires probably meant she should run now, but...

But he's been going to therapy.

But he's been wooing me.

But he's been doing everything I once wished he would.

But I still love him.

And didn't that make her a fool?

At her age, she should know better. Yet here she was, being led through a sex club, about to have wild, kinky sex with her ex-husband, who was blackmailing her into going to couples' therapy with him if she wanted an orgasm.

Is this really my life?

Apparently, it was, and she was the one walking toward almost certain heartbreak, with both eyes wide open. It was the 'almost' that was the problem. If heartbreak was certain, she would have been able to be stronger. Gavin had thrown her off-kilter.

When she'd imagined her future, when she'd imagined growing old, it had always been with him. She could have everything she'd ever wanted, she just had to be willing to risk her heart to the man who had broken it.

They came to a halt in front of a large, padded, leather sex chair. It vaguely resembled a chaise lounge or backless couch, but with a high curve on one side, a low curve on the other, and a deep dip in the middle, and cushions could be added to level out the dip and a head-rest. This particular chair had a multitude of rings along the sides for attaching chains, cuffs, or ropes.

It was one of Leah's favorite pieces of equipment. Heat and need swirled inside her, obscuring the last of her hesitation. It wasn't as if she and Gavin hadn't been doing the physical stuff for years. What harm would another scene do?

Turning to look down at her, Gavin's blue eyes were blazing hot, and there was an intensity to his gaze that took her breath away.

Yeah, they might have been scening together for years without an official relationship, but this was different. She could see it in his eyes, feel it in the tension that circled around them, and knew it deep in her heart.

Such a bad idea.

The thought was too soft, too small against the swirling emotions inside her, the parts of her that were clamoring more loudly.

Touch me.

Pleasure me.

Love me.

Don't let me down again.

Gavin brushed her hair back from her face with gentle fingers as his other hand caressed the back of her neck. His thumb stroked along her jawline. Every tiny touch enhanced the other, a rising tide of teasing sensations that were sensual rather than sexual, yet all of them added to the shimmering need at her core.

"I won't let you down again."

She almost jerked back away from him. She hadn't said that out loud, had she?

No. It was just Gavin, who could sometimes be so in tune with her, as though he was reading her mind. Other times it seemed as if he was so oblivious to what was going on in her head, he might as well have been blind and deaf. Leah had never understood how he managed to do both.

"What's your safe word, love?" he asked, the way he always did at the beginning of a scene with her.

"Hazard."

Ironic, really. She'd chosen it out of amusement, thinking of all the hazards her character encountered during the game, set up by Gavin as the Dungeon Master, but now they were in the real world, and he was still the biggest hazard to her heart.

CHAPTER NINE

GAVIN

There was a bit of uncertainty in Leah's expression, a touch of worry to go along with her arousal and excitement. Exactly what a Dom liked to see, even more so because it had been a long time since he'd seen that particular mix of emotions.

They'd been lovers for so long, they knew what made each other tick. He knew how to touch her, how to caress her, how to pleasure her. There had been a bit of a learning curve as they grew older, but they'd learned together. He knew her body as well as he knew his own, so mutual pleasure was assured.

What was making her uncertain was the emotional element. While he didn't like her unsure of him, he relished the chance to prove himself to her. That he'd stirred her uncertainty, despite her defenses against him, gave him hope.

"Strip," he ordered. "I'll be back in a moment, and I want you naked when I get here."

"Yes, Sir."

One day soon, he promised himself, he'd hear her call him Master again. That was something else he'd lost in the divorce. He'd gotten used to "Sir" over the years, he craved hearing her acknowledge him as *hers* once more.

Several people had already gathered on the edges of the scene area, waiting to see what he and Leah would do. They always had an audience. That was part of the point of the Outlands, but because he was the owner and she was his ex, their audience tended to be on the larger side, no matter what they were doing. Even those who didn't know their past relationship were quickly informed by the other members.

Walking with fast, long strides through the club toward his office where his play bag was, Gavin was aware of Aiden coming up alongside him. The other Dom met his pace, which was good because Gavin wasn't slowing down for him. He knew Leah was perfectly safe where she was, no one would hassle a submissive getting ready for a scene, especially when she already had an audience, but there was a small part of him that worried she'd change her mind if he left her alone for too long.

"Are you sure you know what you're doing?" Aiden asked, keeping his voice even but unable to entirely hide his concern. "I thought you were trying to be different with her this go-round."

"I am, but if she's having sex with me, she's not going to be having sex with anyone else." Gavin gave Aiden a look. Aiden was a bit of a man whore and didn't ascribe to that particular philosophy when he was single—though he had during his two marriages—but he understood that was how Gavin and Leah worked. Even when they weren't married. "Now, if you want to help, go back there and make sure my submissive doesn't run off while I grab my bag."

Shaking his head and muttering under his breath, Aiden reversed directions. Gavin didn't need to look behind him to know Aiden was headed back toward Leah. He would keep an eye on her. While he wouldn't stop her if she truly wanted to leave, he'd slow her down.

Leah

Skin prickling under so many eyes, Leah pretended to ignore everyone as she sank to her knees, naked, and got into her submissive position—knees spread apart, straight back with breasts thrusts out, palms turned up and resting on her thighs, head bowed. Funny how when she'd been younger, she'd been far more worried what everyone would think about her body during a public scene.

She'd been thinner, her curves had been firmer, she hadn't had any cellulite, and her pussy had been pretty, pink, and plump. Now, parts of her sagged, she had wrinkles, dips, and curves, and her belly was far more rounded, yet she felt completely at home in her body. Sure, she had her moments of envy for the young and beautiful, but she had confidence now she'd been missing when she was young and beautiful. She was older and beautiful, though not in the way society often defined beauty.

Remembering how insecure she'd been when her body had been closer to what society thought of as 'beautiful,' she could only shake her head at herself. Back then, all she'd seen were her flaws.

Now she didn't care much about her flaws.

Now she didn't care how many people were looking at her kneeling.

She wasn't entirely comfortable, but that was because this whole kneeling thing was a lot harder on her knees than it used to be.

Should have taken up yoga.

It had also been a long time since Gavin had been unprepared for a scene, so she hadn't spent much time waiting for him in recent years. Their scenes were always scheduled and pre-planned. Doing this spur-of-the-moment added a certain element of anticipation she hadn't anticipated.

Then again, it wasn't as if she'd anticipated scening with Gavin when she'd walked in tonight. She'd come to give him a piece of her mind, at least that's what she'd told herself, but she had a feeling her subconscious had other plans. There was no way she could walk into the Outlands and tell off the Dungeon Master without consequences.

Murmurs from the crowd around her were getting a little louder. Some in impatience with the wait, others...

"Why is he scening with *her?* She's old." The complainer wasn't speaking *that* loudly, but she happened to say it when there was a natural lull in the rest of the noise, making her audible.

Leah turned her head to see a younger woman, probably in her twenties, her hands over her mouth and a horrified look on her face. Her friend, standing next to her, began to edge away, looking just as appalled. At least they were smart enough to know it wasn't acceptable to say such things. Though the way everyone was now staring at them disapprovingly didn't hurt.

Poor babies. That's what they looked like to her—perky breasts, firm curves, perfectly done makeup, probably excited as hell to be in a kink club. She didn't recognize them, which meant they were newer members and had no idea who she was. Undoubtedly, the complaining brunette had a crush on Gavin. It happened all the time.

"So is Master Gavin, honey," she replied, winking at the brunette, who looked like she wanted to sink into the ground. The young woman's face turned even brighter red after Leah responded to her, then Leah's view was blocked as Aiden stepped in front of the young submissive, hands on his hips, probably glaring down at her. Leah couldn't see his expression, but she assumed he was glaring because the young subbie hit her knees so fast, it looked like her legs had collapsed out from under her.

"Be nice, Master Aiden," Leah called out to him, raising her voice a little.

Turning to look over his shoulder, Aiden gave her a half-exasperated, half-disapproving look.

"You handle your business, missy, and I'll handle this. This young subbie needs to be taught some respect." Reaching down, he hauled the brunette to her feet, a sadistic smile curving his lips. "Seems like I might as well be the man to do it since I'm here. Since she likes older men."

The brunette stared up at him, caught somewhere between excitement and terror. Leah pressed her lips together, repressing a smile. From the look in Aiden's eye, he'd found his distraction for the evening. He wouldn't let anyone get away with disrespect—thankfully, Gavin hadn't been around—but he wasn't going to kick her out either, which was what she'd been half-afraid of.

The crowd stirred, and Leah dropped her head down again, looking away from where Aiden was now leading the young woman off. Her heart began to race, all the little hairs on her body lifted, and her skin was beginning to tingle. Gavin had returned. He set down the large duffle bag next to the table there, specifically for whoever was scening at that station.

"Dammit, Leah," he said gruffly, coming to stand in front of her and holding out his hand. "I didn't mean for you to have to kneel the whole time I was away, or I would have told you to kneel."

"I can kneel if I want to, Sir." The tart reply didn't have quite as much impact when she truly couldn't get up without his help. Crap. Was she that out of practice, or was it her joints? Could be either, if she was honest. When she managed to get to her feet with his assistance, she peeked up at him. "It's the getting up I have trouble with, but I still like the kneeling."

"And you do it beautifully, love." He curled his hand under her chin, tilting her head back and lifting her lips for him to brush a kiss over. "But I didn't tell you to kneel. Me, Dom. You, sub. But thank you for giving me a good reason to spank your lovely arse."

As if he wouldn't have found one anyway, but his words still sent a thrill through her. Leah loved a good old-fashioned hand spanking. Her buttocks were already tingling as her body prepared itself for what was to come.

GAVIN

Seeing Leah kneeling and waiting for him had Gavin's emotions in a whirl. Fuck, but he liked the look of it. On the other hand, he'd worried about how long she'd been like that and whether her knees would be able to hold that position.

Now she was flushed and excited, anticipating the punishment he promised, but he wasn't quite ready to give it yet. His brain had been trying to decide what to do with her from the moment she'd requested a scene. Normally, he plotted out their scenes the same way he did campaigns for their group, with lots of preparation for different scenarios and trying to set up a satisfying conclusion.

Unlike with the game campaigns, where she and their friends often went wildly off the course he was trying to direct them on, their kink scenes tended to go as planned. Doing a spontaneous scene was affecting both of them. It felt a little rawer, a little more fraught. They hadn't had time to bolster their usual emotional defenses in anticipation of physical intimacy.

In the past, he would have balked at going into a scene this vulnerable, tried to do something to stir an argument or piss her off, maybe even tried to end the scene. Now, he would embrace it. He was getting a chance to show Leah what he wanted for their future, and he wasn't going to squander it.

"Hands up behind your head," he said. "Stand with your legs apart."

The position lifted her chest, thrusting her breasts out. Her eyes remained on his face, watching him. Gavin let his appreciation for both her quick response and her gorgeous body show.

"Very nice, love." Reaching out, he hefted one of her breasts in his hand, rubbing his thumb over her nipple. Leah sighed with pleasure, leaning into the caress, her eyes going a bit hazy. "Now bend over, as best you can."

The look she shot him was scornful.

"I'm not *that* old."

Lifting his hand, Gavin gave the side of her breast a short, sharp slap, making her gasp. She lifted slightly, not quite going up on her toes, before settling back down, a pretty flush in her cheeks from the little bite of pain.

"Don't forget to call me Sir… or Master." He tacked the latter on as an afterthought, though it felt anything but. Gavin hadn't asked her to call him Master since the divorce. Requesting it now, well, it meant something to him, and from the way her eyes widened in shock, he knew it meant something to her as well.

Maybe just the fact he'd set himself up for possible public rejection at her hands meant something to her. Her expression smoothed out, but he could see the uncertainty lingering in her eyes.

"I'm not *that* old, *Sir.*" She bent at the waist, hiding her face from him as her hair fell down on either side of her head. To back up her words, she didn't seem to have any trouble standing with her torso parallel to the ground.

Gavin hid a smile. He could see quite a few members of their audience grinning in appreciation of her sass, especially the other women around her age.

Going to his toy bag, he grabbed the case where he kept the plugs and lube. His expectations were rising along with his cock—this was going to be a good night.

CHAPTER TEN

Despite her bravado, Leah wasn't sure how long she would be able to hold this position. She definitely needed to start working out again. On the other hand, pure stubbornness would keep her in place for far longer than she probably wanted. She didn't think Gavin would have her bent over here for too long. Not when there was a bondage sex chair right next to them, waiting for an occupant.

In her position, she couldn't see what he was doing, but when he got something from his bag and walked around behind her, she was willing to bet it had something to do with her ass. A moment later, his hand pressed against the small of her back, and something cold, hard, and slick touched her anus.

Really? No warmup or anything, just straight for my butt?

Anything anal always made her feel as if she was doing something she shouldn't be, which turned her on. Yet she couldn't stifle her whimper when he pushed the plug in, slow and steady. It wasn't a very large plug, but it wasn't the smallest he had. Long, tapered, and thick enough to burn when the widest part approached the tight ring of her entrance. Leah panted, doing her best not to shift her weight as he filled her.

Apparently, it didn't matter how old she got. There was still a little part of her that primly felt only bad girls took it in the ass. Perversely, feeling like a bad girl only made her more aroused. Her muscles clenched around the toy filling her, and she gasped when Gavin twisted the base, spinning it inside of her and lighting up all the little nerve endings surrounding it.

It shouldn't feel so good, but it always did. Good. Wrong. Hot. Degrading. Arousing. Everything at once.

Gavin didn't usually start out a scene going straight for her ass because he knew the effect anal had on her, so she couldn't help but wonder if he was deliberately trying to shake things up for them or if he was completely winging it.

"My bonny lass," he murmured, tugging gently on the plug, so it pressed against the inside of her entrance. Leah whimpered again. Her legs and core muscles were starting to feel the burn of her position more now, but she didn't want him to stop. She'd been bent over in front of him like this so many times, but it never seemed to lose its appeal for either of them.

Leah whimpered, wriggling slightly, and Gavin let go of the plug, giving her bottom a nice, sharp smack. The pain reverberated through her, mingling with the pleasure from being filled by the plug, and Leah moaned. Yes, this was what she'd wanted—needed—w

when she'd decided to storm into the Outlands tonight. What she'd hoped Gavin would give her.

"Stand up straight, love." His hand caressed the spot he'd swatted as he gave the order, soothing the burn he'd ignited.

Feeling almost dizzy from the combination of holding her position and her needy arousal, she didn't protest when he gently helped her stand straight, his hands assisting to steady her balance. The muscles of her stomach and legs wanted to sag in relief.

"Thank you, Sir," she said automatically. Even though a little part of her pride was pricked when she needed help to do something so simple these days, she still appreciated that Gavin always stepped in to assist without asking. It made her feel cared about.

"Good girl."

The accolade warmed her from the inside out, the way it always did. When she was younger, she'd felt conflicted whenever she was praised with what should have felt like patronizing approval. Now, she loved being called a good girl because that's what she wanted to be... unless she was in the mood to be a naughty girl. Her ass clenched around the plug at the thought. It made her feel naughty, yet it was a reminder to be good at the same time.

Would he go for anal sex? That was normally reserved for funishment sessions, so she was unsure how he planned for tonight to go. The inability to guess his intentions ramped up her anxiety and excitement.

GAVIN

Returning to his bag, Gavin turned his head enough to watch Leah's reaction as he pulled out the long length of silky red rope, neatly bundled together. Her tongue darted out to lick nervously at her lower lip, her face showing her surprise, and he grinned. Nice to know she hadn't guessed he'd be using the rope tonight.

He wasn't a Shibari master, but he knew the basics well enough to put her in a pretty rope dress with some conveniently placed knots.

Undoing the knot keeping the rope bundled together, Gavin walked back toward her, pulling the rope free and readying it for use. She didn't react outwardly, but he could tell Leah was practically wriggling with excitement and apprehension. With that length of rope, he could pretty much do as he pleased.

"Let me know if anything feels too tight," he reminded her as he started to wrap her in the rope.

"Yes, Sir."

Over, under, around... Leah's breathing began to even out as he looped the rope around her neck and began to tie the knots at various points down the front of her before he looped the rest of it around her. When he ran the tail up between her legs to the small loop at her back, she moaned and rocked her hips forward, making him grin widely. The last knot on her front was perfectly positioned against her clit, and now that he had the tail pulled through, it would press that sensitive nubbin as well as pushing against the base of her plug. Which was exactly why the first thing he'd done was plug her.

Still, she knew better than that.

Gavin smacked her ass, the opposite cheek from the one he'd swatted last time.

"Naughty girl, stay still," he warned. A soft whimper was her only response, but her quivering quieted again.

Separating the ropes at her back, he moved around to her front again, crossing them over her body. The rope began to frame her breasts and her stomach, ending just above her hips. Leah sighed as he finished tying her off. Seeing the red rope against her pale skin, the way she held so very still for him, his cock throbbed in response.

When they were younger, he had her kneel at this point to suck him off, so he could regain his control before moving on. Now that he was older, he didn't always have two rounds in him, and his self-control was far greater than it had been in his youth. Though, for old time's sake...

Unbuckling the sides of his kilt with quick ease born of long familiarity with the process, he tossed the fabric onto the low end of the sex chair. He'd move it later if he needed to.

His cock jutted out in front of him, hard and heavy. Gavin had begun shaving years ago when the grey started coming in, which had the happy side effect of making him look even bigger. Leah's gaze had dropped down to his groin. Knowing she was looking at him made his blood throb as he grew even larger.

"On your knees again, love."

Leah lowered herself down, letting her hands drop to her thighs. Gavin reached out to sweep her hair up into two hands, pulling it to the back of her head in a ponytail. It took him less than a moment before he was using it to guide her forward. Her lips parted, and she took him between them, making him groan as the silky heat of her mouth engulfed his cock.

She knew exactly how to rub her tongue along his shaft, the sensitive spot beneath the mushroom head that always made him shudder, and the way he liked to have her slide all the way down, then suck hard as she pulled back. Tightening his grip on her hair as he wrestled with his own self-control, he watched her smoothly move her lips over his shaft, her head bobbing back and forth. The expression on her face was almost peaceful, the combination of the rope dress bondage and servicing a Dom having a palpable effect on her.

"Such a pretty cocksucker," he murmured appreciatively, enjoying the humming vibrations of her pleased response. Damn him, but she was beautiful. He never got tired of the sight of her on her knees before him, but this isn't where he wanted to spend himself.

Allowing himself to enjoy the leisurely blowjob for a few more long, pleasurable minutes, Gavin finally tugged her away, reluctantly leaving the sweet warmth of her mouth.

"Up, love. It's time for your punishment."

Her eyes lit up with anticipation.

Leah

Mouth still watering from the blow job, Leah felt a little woozy, a little drunk on pleasure. High on it, even. Gavin wasn't following the normal sequence of events their scenes followed, which was throwing her off and exciting her.

While she'd had his cock in her mouth, her ass had been squeezing around the plug, reveling in the sensation of being filled at both ends, and her needy pussy had been left empty. It wasn't untouched. The rope wedged between her lips was getting wetter and wetter from her slickness. She doubted they'd need the lube tonight, though Gavin would likely use some anyway, just in case.

Every time she shifted position, the knot pressing against her clit shifted as well, rubbing against her most sensitive spot and teasing her. It wasn't nearly enough to get her off, but it was more than enough to frustrate and stimulate.

Again, Gavin helped her to her feet before pulling her hair back and using a hairband he'd had on his wrist to secure it in a ponytail behind her head. He'd gone back to his toy bag for nipple clamps and a leather paddle.

Setting the paddle down on the sex chair, he moved to her front, cupping one of her breasts in his hand. Her nipples were already standing at attention, dark pink and eager to be tormented. The clamps he held were her favorite, rubber-tipped and spring-loaded; they'd pinch hard enough to bite but wouldn't be unduly harsh. Her pussy clenched in anticipation, and she had to fight the urge to wriggle to shift the knot against her clit.

Gavin's blue eyes bore into hers, alight with the anticipation of erotically torturing her. While she wouldn't call him a full-on sadist, he certainly had a streak, and she was masochistic enough to love it.

Holding her gaze, so he could watch the change in her expression, he cupped her breast, squeezing it gently before applying the clamp. Leah sucked in a breath, trapped by his eyes and unable to look away, even as the sharp pinch of pain swept through her. Her nipple throbbed in protest against the tight confines of the clamp, then she slowly let out her breath as the sharpness of the initial pinch faded to a more manageable pulsing pain.

The inner muscles of her pussy were fluttering in time with the way her ass clenched around the plug, sending slow waves of hot arousal flowing through her, mingling with the erotic torture and creating entirely new sensations. The endorphins were sending her higher and higher. Then he added the second clamp.

Leah moaned, shuddering at the first hot flash of pain, followed by the slow, smooth roll of pleasure that spread through her like molasses being poured through her veins. Her nipples throbbed, twin points of pain on her chest, while her need coiled in her lower belly. Her clit throbbed, too, swollen and aching for more touch, while the steady pressure of the knot against it kept pressing and pressing, similar to the way the clamps kept their steady grip but without the painful element.

"Good girl. Now let's get you positioned over the chair, love."

Bent over with the leather paddle in front of her, the rope between her legs felt even tighter, shoving the plug deeper inside her and rubbing more firmly against her clit. Gavin had positioned her over the high end of the chair, arranging her like a doll before wrapping leather restraints around her wrists and ankles, attaching them to the chair, spreading her legs and arms wide.

Her body was supported by the upper curve, which meant her breasts and nipples were pressing against the leather unless she arched her back to relieve the pressure on her clamped nipples. That position was not only uncomfortable and hard to hold, it tightened all the ropes and rubbed the knot against her clit in a painful manner. As predicament bondage went, it wasn't the worst, but it was delightfully devious.

She knew once he started spanking her, and her body reacted, it was only going to get worse.

CHAPTER ELEVEN

GAVIN

Laid out in front of him, restraints on her limbs, rope around her body, and her pretty arse tipped up in the air, waiting for his hand and the paddle, Leah was a dream come true. He could look at her all day long, tied up pretty and waiting for him. The dark pink shell between her legs was slicker than he'd anticipated, wetting the rope between her pouting lips.

Carefully, he rubbed his fingers around the knot over her clit, and she moaned, lifting her hips, then shuddering as the rope shifted against her tender flesh. Reaching down with his other hand, he gave his cock a hard stroke, already missing the feel of her mouth around him.

Well, the faster he finished tormenting her, the faster he could fuck her. He had been enjoying taking his time, but it was getting harder to take things slowly—pun not intended, despite how hard his dick was.

"Ready, naughty girl?" he asked, trailing his fingers over the soft skin of her buttocks, her pretty cheeks bisected by the rope. He didn't intend to match her skin to the bright red of the rope, but he might get it pretty close. Between his hand and the leather paddle, it wouldn't be difficult.

"Yes, Sir," she replied automatically, shivering. Leah liked being called a 'naughty girl' as much as she did a 'good girl.' Gavin did his best to oblige by calling her both when they were scening... he also did his best not to overuse them.

"Do ye understand why ye are being punished?" He knew his brogue was thickening as he caressed her cheeks, anticipation licking through him and coming out in his speech.

Leah sighed.

"Because I knelt like a very proper submissive, even though you hadn't told me to."

That was his sassy lass. Gavin spanked her thigh, just under her buttock, knowing it would both surprise her and hurt more. She shrieked, jerking, then moaned at the effect her movement had on the ropes before settling back down into position.

"That's right, love. Don't try to anticipate your Dom. Wait until you've been given an order."

Rather than waiting for her reply, if she was going to make one, Gavin brought his hand down hard on the upturned curve of her bottom and began her spanking in earnest. Leah cried out again, back arching, then moaned, her head dropping submissively as he swatted her backside. Not too harshly, but not gently either, making sure to cover each cheek thoroughly so she'd be feeling it all over.

Leah

Whimpering and doing her best not to wriggle too much, Leah panted as Gavin rained down crisp swats against her soft flesh.

Ow, ow, ow.

It hurt. Spankings always hurt, but somehow, her body took the stinging pain, the sharp burn, and morphed it into something different. It wasn't pleasure, exactly—it still hurt—but at the same time, it felt good.

Not just physically.

The domination, the helplessness of her position, Gavin's complete control over her all fed into her arousal as much as the punishment. The hot burn from the spanking sank into her, stoking the heat at her core, making her burn hotter and wetter between her legs. The more it hurt, the more she had to take for him, the more submissive she felt. Her nipples throbbed, her pussy and ass clenched, and her hands tugged uselessly at the restraints as he kept spanking her.

With so many sensations coursing through her, mixing together, it was easy to let all her worries, all her frustrations go. Her brain couldn't hold on to those when she was completely distracted, trying to find a position that wasn't too painful on her nipples or clit while Gavin turned her ass pink.

By the time he picked up the paddle, her ass felt hot all over, and she moaned as the leather implement was lifted. Anticipation? Protest? A little bit of both. Her skin was already painfully hot, yet she craved more. Needed it.

The paddle crashed down on her ass, and she shrieked. Gavin's hand was hard, but the paddle was much harder and covered more territory, leaving a burning swath of flesh in its wake. Her clamped nipples rubbed against the leather as she writhed, and the knotted rope rubbed almost painfully against her swollen clit as her ass tightened around the plug.

Fire licked over her skin as Gavin laid down another swat with the paddle, just under the first one.

It hurt. It hurt so good... so bad... it didn't matter. They were one and the same. From experience, she knew she would still feel this spanking tomorrow morning, which was likely Gavin's design, but that thought was small and quiet against the exquisite agony wreaking havoc with her senses.

Another blow, smacking against the undercurve of her ass, and Leah's toes curled. The long blade of the paddle caught both cheeks, and where it landed, slapped against her swollen pussy lips and the base of the plug in her ass. Her sensitive labia stung, and she could feel the reverberations deep inside, thanks to the plug.

"Good girl." Gavin's approval sank into her like a wave of warmth, coating her from the inside out with satisfaction.

Hard hands gripped her reddened cheeks, squeezing firmly enough to make her moan again as the sting was reignited by his rough handling.

More, more, more.

He released her, and Leah wanted to wail with the loss of contact. She panted, waiting. Her pussy quivered with hope.

Time for orgasms?

The tension on her ankles gave out, and the part of her brain still functioning cheered. They'd be going back to Gavin's office now, where he'd fuck her senseless, and she would have all the orgasms she could handle.

He moved beside her and unclipped the wrist restraints from the chair. Strong arms helped her up, surprising her when he lifted her against him. When they were younger, he carried her just like this all the time. As they got older, it had become more sporadic, especially after the divorce.

Unfortunately, Leah didn't really have time to appreciate it because he was already lowering her down... onto the sex chair. Her muzzy thoughts were slow to catch up, but her confusion came on fast enough.

"What—"

Gavin's eyes blazed as he propped her with her back up against the high curve, settling her there while his fingers reached behind her. The rope between her legs went slack, then she could feel the head of his cock press up against her pussy. It was slick enough she could tell he'd used lube over his shaft at some point before getting her onto the chair.

Shocked, she stared back at him.

They never fucked in public.

Well, not never, but not since the divorce. After each scene, Gavin would sweep her away to his office as if she was his dirty little secret.

They'd fuck like bunnies, but never in front of people. It wasn't on her hard limits or even her soft. Leah didn't mind being watched.

She just never expected to be anymore.

His hand splayed over her groin, thumb slipping between the lips of her pussy and pressing as he thrust into her, filling her. Gasping, Leah arched, her hands automatically coming up to push against his chest, her inner muscles tightening as she sank down onto him. All around them, she could hear murmurs of surprise—long-time members who also hadn't expected the scene to keep going.

Gavin was taking her in front of all of them—the same way he had when they'd been *together* together—a public re-claiming with witnesses.

Fuck!

GAVIN

He hadn't planned to have sex in public tonight. In the back of his head, he'd assumed it would be the same as always, but some impulse deep inside him wanted to switch things up. To make it different. To make Leah understand that this wasn't going to be business as usual.

She might have come into the club to face off with him, to push him into giving her the scene she wanted, but they were doing things on *his* terms now. There would be no hiding the change in their relationship from everyone else. No waiting to see if she accepted him back into her life before he declared his intentions.

If things went to shit again, everyone would know. It was the most vulnerable he'd ever made himself, and he could tell it shocked her even more than when he'd told their friends he wanted to get back together with her.

Lowering his lips, he kissed her deeply as he began to rock his hips. The chair's positioning meant she was sort of on top of him but still under his control. One hand on her hip, the other still positioned so he could rub her clit in slow circles, held her in place while he moved, pressing her against the chair's back.

Her fingers massaged his chest muscles, her head falling back when he released her lips, baring her throat to him. He kissed his way down, thrusting and grinding against her clit the whole way. The trail of rope that had been between her legs now hung down from the rope dress, draping over his leg and tickling him in a somewhat distracting manner.

Leah whimpered beneath him, squirming when his chest pushed against her breasts. Her pink nipples were red, still trapped in the grip of the clamps. She shuddered when Gavin used the chair to push her a little further up, allowing him to suck one into his mouth, clamp and all, while he continued to impale her on his cock.

"Gavin!" Her nails dug into him, and he moved harder, faster, feeling her pussy quivering around him as her orgasm approached. His tongue swept over the exposed tip of her nipple, and he sucked hard.

Crying out, Leah clung to him, shuddering and clenching around him. She was already tighter than usual, thanks to the plug, but when she came, her muscles clamped down in a stranglehold on his cock.

He leaned into her, making small movements with his hips as he released her nipple from his lips, moving his hand, so he could rub his pubic bone against her clit, drawing another cry from her lips as she spasmed with the sweet ecstasy of her release.

Sliding his hand up her ribs to her breast, he removed the clamp he'd been sucking on, and Leah shrieked as the blood rushed back into the tortured bud.

Leah

The tumult of sensations cascading through her body was a heady mix of pain and pleasure, so overwhelming it was becoming impossible to tell which was which. Her brain interpreted it all the same.

The release of one nipple, then the other from the clamps, made her pulse pound in her ears. Gavin's large body pressed against hers, his mouth covering her lips, claiming them for another kiss and trapping her between him and the back of the chair. Leah wrapped her legs and arms around him, clinging to him as if he was her anchor in the storm of passion that threatened to drown her.

Ecstasy poured through her in waves, pain and pleasure swirling inside her as his chest moved against hers, abrading her nipples, his cock filling her over and over, body rocking against her clit. The hard thrusts bounced her ass off the chair, sparking a delicious new burn where she'd been spanked.

"*Mo chridhe...*" He moaned the words, and Leah screamed as another bout of rapture wracked her senses.

Hearing the endearment while they were having sex in the middle of the Outlands... The past and the present were colliding, breaking down the barriers that had been between them, shattering her defenses, and tears sparked in her eyes. Right now, it felt real.

It all felt so real.

And she didn't want to lose it again.

CHAPTER TWELVE

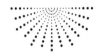

LEAH

She woke up fast and hard, her brain pinging her that something was different. Not wrong, but different. She wasn't in her own bed, for one, and there was someone else *in* bed with her.

Simon?

No. Of course not. The little spots of pain all over her body and the feeling of being completely satiated told her that.

She'd had a date with Simon, but she'd ended her night with Gavin. Like the nincompoop she was.

Mistakes... I've made a few...

Was it a mistake?

As the events of last night came back to her, like a film reel playing out to her conscious mind now that she was fully awake, she had to admit she wasn't sure. She'd gone into the Outlands expecting it to be like any other scene from the past decade, thinking in the back of her mind it would be like setting a reset button on how she viewed Gavin.

There'd be pain, pleasure, then they'd end the evening by going their separate ways, the way they always did, and everything would feel the same way it had for years.

Except that wasn't what happened.

She'd hit a level of submission she hadn't allowed in years. Subconsciously she hadn't trusted Gavin enough to give her submission in years, but last night, her subconscious defenses had apparently decided to fuck off, and he got in her head. The pleasure had been greater, but so were the repercussions.

There had been no way she could have driven herself home last night, so instead of driving her there, Gavin had taken her to his condo. It wasn't the first time she'd been here, they'd occasionally scened here as well, but it was the first time in years she'd slept over.

"The first time in years" was apparently her new mantra, and she wasn't sure she liked it. Right now, she felt raw, and not just her body parts. Last night, Gavin had done more than make himself vulnerable. He'd exposed all the wounded parts of her she'd kept shielded for so long and touched them.

The urge to get away and hide was so strong, it left her choked up and breathless as if she couldn't get enough air down her throat and into her lungs. Panic clawing its way up her chest, she squirmed away from the muscled arm around her waist, the hot body pressing into her back.

Who knew getting everything she wanted could be so scary?

Maybe because you don't know if you're getting everything you want yet. It just feels like you could. You also know that means risking losing it all over again.

Yeah, that sounded right.

Crap, she needed to get out of here. She needed time and space to process. She also needed to get home to Oliver. Her poor kitty had now been left alone all night twice in the past few weeks. At least she was partially dressed. Somehow, she'd ended up in one of Gavin's shirts rather than the dress she'd been wearing for her date last night and no underwear. She didn't want to think about how much she *didn't* want to take off Gavin's shirt.

Why were men's shirts so much more comfortable than her own? Not 'men' as in all men's clothes, but when something belonged to a *specific* man, somehow it became softer and more comfortable...

Oh my God, get yourself together and get out of here.

Sliding off the bed, she let out a very soft sigh of relief when she managed it without waking Gavin. Lying on his side, no longer curled around her, he still maintained the position he'd been in when she'd been snuggled up beside him. Thank goodness he was still a deep sleeper. He still looked so good in his sleep. Older than the young man she'd fallen in love with, but when she'd been young and imagining the future, she'd pictured waking up to this every morning.

Something inside her softened yet panicked at the same time. Yeah, she needed to get out of here. The yearning in her heart was becoming a little scary, and she needed to get that under control before she decided her next move.

Thankfully, her phone was on the nightstand. Gavin had driven them here last night since she'd been too out of it to demand to be taken home. Either way, her car would have been at the Outlands, so she would have needed a ride over there. Waking *him* up to give her a ride... yeah, no.

Most awkward morning after ever.

Quickly shooting off a text to Cyana, she asked if she was up and could pick her up from Gavin's—wincing slightly at the scolding she was sure would be coming her way, but that's exactly *why* she'd texted Cyana. Not only did Esther have kids and Jax to contend with on the weekend mornings, she also tended to be a little more romantic and a little more forgiving. Cyana was the hardass.

She'd be the best at helping Leah decide if she was making a huge mistake. Sugarcoating things was not part of her personality, which was what Leah needed right now—a reality check. Her own judgment couldn't be trusted. Her judgment had sent her to the Outlands last night, where she'd not only scened with Gavin but had let down her guard against him further than she could countenance, then gone home with him and slept all night in his bed.

Yup. She was not to be trusted. That's for sure.

Relief and gratitude swept through her when Cyana texted her back almost immediately, saying she was on her way. She'd probably literally dropped everything she was doing after getting the text.

"What are ye doing?"

The thick Scottish brogue rolling Gavin's 'r' seemed even thicker than usual. Leah froze, turning her head to see him blinking at her from the bed.

Shit. Caught.

GAVIN

Even as he asked, Gavin knew the answer. Running. She was running. Again. Just like she had in the past. Hurt and anger rose up, and he barely managed to tamp it down. He always woke up grouchy, and there was a part of him that knew he wasn't being fair.

He'd talked with Dr. Silverwood about this. He saw it as Leah running and refusing to work things out, but he'd had to acknowledge, Leah *had* tried to work things out before she left. He just hadn't known what the stakes were... because she hadn't told him.

That's what they were going to work on and why they were going to Dr. Silverwood this week. Together.

Memory of that triumph soothed the hurt and anger. He let them go. They were a reaction and not a particularly useful one in this instance. Besides, he'd somewhat anticipated this when he'd made the decision to bring her home with him, but he hadn't been able to help himself. She'd been in no shape to drive her own car, and taking her home and leaving her there by herself had felt impossible. He'd also known she'd be even more upset if he invaded *her* space, and they woke up together in her bed.

"I, uh..." Her gaze flitted away from his, eyes averting. Cell phone in one hand, her fingers on the other hand, plucking nervously at the hem of his shirt—he did like seeing her wearing his shirt again—she resembled a startled deer. "I need to go."

"Alright. I'll take you back to the Outlands."

"Right... um." Her grip tightened on her phone. "You don't have to. I have a ride."

"Cancel it. There's no point in someone going out of their way when I can take you straight there." He was countering with logic, but the truth was, he wasn't quite ready to let her go yet. Didn't want her retreating until he was able to have some kind of final say.

"Oh... well, right, that makes sense." She muttered something under her breath he couldn't quite hear, but he was pretty sure it was a curse word.

Amused, Gavin got out of bed, pretending he didn't notice her texting while he got dressed, pretending he didn't notice the appreciative glances she kept shooting him. He did notice and preened a little. Might not be as young as he once was, but he was proud of the shape he kept himself in.

He knew he was looking back at her the same way. Fuck, but he'd missed seeing her in the mornings, blonde hair mussed and falling in waves around her shoulders, cheeks pink, and he really couldn't emphasize enough how much he liked seeing her in his shirt again.

"Do you want to change?" he asked casually, hoping the answer was no. "I have some pants you can wear if you don't want to wear your dress from last night."

"Pants would be great, thanks." Her cheeks turned a little pinker, and Gavin grinned as he reached into one of his drawers to get a pair of pants that were a little tight on him after shrinking in the wash. They had a drawstring, so they'd fit her well enough. He could only hope the reason she agreed was she didn't want to give up his clothes. If he lost a couple items of clothing to her today, he'd be thrilled.

"Do you want breakfast? Coffee?" he asked, handing her the pants. Leah kept avoiding his gaze, and inwardly, he sighed. At least she was taking his clothes. He'd count that as a win.

"Um, no, I'll eat when I get home. Sorry, I have a lot to do today."

Liar, liar, the pants he'd just given her were already on fire. Gavin didn't call her on it. She needed space after last night, and even though it killed him, he knew he needed to give it to her. One step at a time. They'd scened together, she'd slept over at his house, was wearing his clothes home, and going to therapy with him on Wednesday.

Actually, when he thought about it like that, this wasn't so bad. Feeling slightly cheered, he finished getting dressed. By the time he was done, Leah was fidgeting, frowning slightly at whatever thoughts were running through her busy brain.

The frown was something he could do without.

"How's your arse," he asked, coming up alongside her and cupping the anatomy in question.

Squeaking, Leah slapped at his hand, shifting away. Her cheeks were even hotter. "It's fine!"

Chuckling, Gavin stepped away. Well, at least she wasn't frowning anymore. Blushing, but also hiding a smile. Much better.

LEAH

The car ride back to the Outlands was thankfully short and not nearly as awkward as she'd worried it would be. Gavin put the radio on and didn't try to make conversation; he hummed along with the songs instead. Leah shifted in her seat, only a little uncomfortable. Last night's spanking lingered, and her nipples were still sore, both things a lot more noticeable now that she wasn't focused on trying to sneak out the door without waking Gavin.

She hadn't expected him to be flirtatiously good-humored this morning. He was grouchy in the morning at the best of times, and after waking up and catching her on her way out the door, she figured there'd be a blow-up.

Instead, he had her as off-kilter as he had the night before.

Dammit. She really could have used Cyana's reality check.

Pulling up alongside her car, Gavin smiled at her with a smugness that made her itch to smack him. He knew he'd gotten under her skin, and it was making her feel extra defensive—both the fact he'd gotten under her skin and that he knew it. The big jerk.

"I'll see you on Wednesday then?"

Crap. Right. Wednesday, when she'd agreed to go to therapy with him. The small space inside the car felt as if it was getting smaller. She was walking down a road she wasn't sure she wanted to travel again, but she couldn't seem to find a good offramp, but she'd agreed.

She did want to know what a therapist had to say. Maybe she'd finally be able to vent everything and let all her emotions go.

"Yes, text me the details," she said, nodding and getting out of the car before he could do anything like lean in and try to kiss her.

So why was she so disappointed when he waved his hand and drove off as soon as she was in her own car?

CHAPTER THIRTEEN

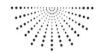

LEAH

Cyana and Esther were waiting for her outside her house, even though she'd texted Cyana and told her she didn't actually need a ride anymore. To be honest, she'd kinda figured Cyana would either call or show up, but Esther was a surprise. Not a bad one.

Seeing them, a sense of relief swept over her. Esther probably *would* be more encouraging about getting back together with Gavin than Cyana, she valued both of their opinions. Besides, now that she thought about it, if Esther wasn't supportive, that would be *extremely* telling.

"I should have known you'd show up here," Leah called out, getting out of the car shaking her head.

"Nice morning after look," Cyana responded, cracking a smile. "Rock that walk of shame, baby!" As always, she managed to look put-together, even wearing yoga pants and a slouchy shirt, with her silvery hair straightened and brushing against the tops of her shoulders. She was even wearing makeup.

Next to her, Esther was also wearing yoga pants and a t-shirt, but she appeared frazzled next to Cyana. Her dark hair was pulled up into a messy bun, and her shirt wasn't that different from Cyana's—

though it did have writing on it and Cyana's was plain—and she was wearing similar pants, but somehow, she looked messier. Leah sighed inwardly. She had a feeling, in Gavin's oversized clothes, she made both of them look good by comparison.

"Heels and sweatpants. I like it." Esther grinned. She was holding two cups of takeout coffee and held one out to Leah as she approached.

"Thank you, you're a lifesaver," Leah said, moaning when the smell hit her olfactory system. *Good. Want. Need.* They must have been waiting for a bit because it had thankfully cooled down enough for her to take an immediate sip.

"We brought breakfast, too." Cyana held up a bag from the local bagel place. "Figured you'd need some fuel before your interrogation."

"Do you have to call it that?" Leah complained, but she couldn't help smiling. She hadn't known that was coming, with both of them standing here. She opened the front door, letting them in. Oliver came running straight to her, his loud meows a clear demand for breakfast. Leah picked him up and nuzzled the top of his head. "Sorry, baby."

"You were supposed to be on a date with Simon last night. Instead, you clearly ended up making the beast with two backs with Gavin… so, yes." Esther walked by her, giving her a *Significant Look.*

"Just call it sex, Pollyanna." Shaking her head, Cyana followed Esther into the kitchen, so they could sit down at the little table and started pulling out the breakfasts while Leah fed Oliver. It turned out he was far more interested in the food than her and immediately dug in.

They'd been friends for long enough, Cyana had known to get Leah an 'everything' bagel with cream cheese, lox, onions, and capers. It was comfort food as far as she was concerned and exactly what she needed after last night.

Both of her friends noted her wince when she sat down a little too fast on the hard wood chair. *Ouch.* Yeah, she'd forgotten about the state of her butt. The lingering burn wasn't enough to be noticeable until she sat down, especially when there wasn't a cushion.

"So…" Cyana unwrapped her own breakfast, identical to Leah's. Esther was the odd woman out with a breakfast bagel sandwich that smelled amazing. "Anyone do anything interesting last night?"

They both looked at Leah. Sighing inwardly, Leah gave them the rundown. At least she had her delicious, salty lox bagel to make her feel better.

"Wait, *in* the club? He had sex with you *in* the club, not in his office?" Esther looked almost starry-eyed. She knew what a big deal that was. They all did. Of course, she locked onto it.

"Yes. I feel like he's caging me in. Telling all of you. Telling our son. Making things public at the club." Irritation rose. Even having to admit to her friends everything that had happened last night played into his hand. He was making it very, very difficult for her to turn him away.

"Or setting himself up for a massively public rejection," Cyana pointed out, raising one perfectly arched brow. "You don't *have* to take him back. No one would blame you if you didn't."

"Won't they?" Her voice came out a little plaintive, and she realized that might be her big problem. She *was* worried they would blame her. Gavin was giving her everything she'd said she wanted in the past—therapy, open communication, showing himself to be vulnerable—so if she turned that down…

"No, they won't, but if anyone does, they're a jackass whose opinion doesn't matter, anyway. Just because someone says all the right things does all the right things doesn't mean they're the right one for you. You're not a machine where if you put in all the right data, the desired result appears. You're a human being, and you get a say in what you want out of your future. Anyone who says differently isn't worth listening to." Cyana's point, delivered in her usual firm tone, was everything Leah needed to hear.

She felt a little less trapped. Unfortunately, she didn't feel any more certain about what she should do. Knowing her friends wouldn't judge her if she didn't give in to Gavin took off some of the pressure.

"Do you think he's doing all this to trap you?" Esther asked, her brow furrowed. Leah could tell she was doing her best to keep her disbelief out of her tone, but some of it still trickled through. Cyana snorted and shook her head, making her own opinion very clear.

There was a paranoid part of Leah that thought she might not put it past him, but considering Cyana's point about how many people would know he'd been rejected if things didn't work out.... Yeah, she couldn't see Gavin risking his pride to manipulate her. There were a million other ways that didn't have such a high risk of embarrassment for him and were a lot subtler.

Instead, he'd come on strong and publicly.

"No." She sighed. "But I feel a little trapped. Knowing you two aren't judging me for being wary helps."

"It took a long time for your marriage to fall apart," Cyana said. "It'll take a while to put it back together, if it can be. If it's not right, don't get back into it."

"You are so cynical," Esther scolded, then turned to Leah. "I am absolutely not going to judge you if you don't want to get back together with him in the end, but I won't lie, I hope you give him a chance. I don't think you'd be this conflicted about things if you didn't really want to see what happens."

Well, that hit the point right on the nose.

"Ugh. I hate it when you're right. Both of you." Leah took an aggressive bite out of her bagel. "I wish I knew more of what was going on in his head, but I guess I'll find out in therapy." Cyana and Esther exchanged a glance. "What?"

"Maybe before that." Cyana shrugged, her face lighting up with a grin. "Esther and I sent over spies this morning."

GAVIN

The authoritative knocking on Gavin's door was immediately followed by Aiden's deep voice.

"Breakfast delivery! Open up!"

Another deep voice murmured something to Aiden, but not loudly enough for Gavin to hear through the door. Shaking his head, he strode over and opened it. Jax and Aiden were standing on the other side, holding big plastic bags, and something smelled delicious.

"A wee bit early for the gym today," he said dryly. They usually went together in the Sunday afternoons, although Jax had missed a few workouts recently. Since he had Esther and the kids, his schedule was a little harder to pin down. Aiden was in sweatpants and a t-shirt, but Jax was wearing jeans, making Gavin wonder if this was going to be another missed workout.

"I'm not going to make it to the gym today," Jax said, shouldering his way through the door as if in answer to Gavin's thoughts. "We've been sent over here on a reconnoitering mission, but I have to leave in an hour."

Gavin raised his eyebrows. Wow. Esther moved fast. He hadn't expected to be bearded in his own den today, but he wouldn't have been surprised if Jax questioned him during gym time.

"What's your excuse?" he asked Aiden.

"Cyana called me and told me to get my ass over here with Jax." The big man put down the bag he was carrying on Gavin's counter and pulled out the plastic containers inside. They'd gone protein-heavy on the food, lots of sausage, bacon, and eggs to get them started, though Jax pulled out a container of pancakes as well. Gavin's mouth watered.

"And you listened?" That didn't sound like Aiden.

"I was too curious not to."

That did sound like Aiden. Ordering him to do anything was always a risk. There was every likelihood he would do the opposite just to be ornery.

Sitting at the table to eat, it wasn't the company Gavin had hoped to have this morning, but it was a relief not to be on his own. He likely would have spent all morning moping about Leah's swift exit if his friends hadn't shown up.

"I've caught Jax up on last night until you and Leah left the club," Aiden said, getting the ball rolling. "What happened after?"

"She was flying high in subspace, so I brought her back here. We slept—actually slept. This morning, she bolted as fast as she could." He gave the rundown as matter-of-factly as he could, automatically doing his best to hide the hurt her quick exit had stirred. He'd understood it but hadn't liked it. "On Wednesday, she'll be going to see my therapist with me."

"Impressive." Jax looked a little surprised. "I thought it would take her a lot longer to agree to do that."

"Well, apparently, I ruined her date last night." Gavin shrugged. That part he wasn't at all unhappy about. Jax and Aiden frowned at him.

"You didn't show up right before it again, did you?" Aiden squinted at him, almost suspiciously.

"Hell, no!" He cleared his throat. "I may have shown up in the morning with some stuff for her hangover."

"Nice." Aiden held out his hand to be fist-bumped. Rolling his eyes, Gavin bumped his knuckles against Aiden's. The gesture itself made him feel weird and old, but he appreciated the support. Jax's mouth twitched in amusement, and he shook his head.

"It would have been nicer if she hadn't run out this morning like a banshee with her hair on fire."

"I'm surprised you aren't more ticked off about that," Jax said. He was studying Gavin intently, which wasn't the most comfortable position to be in. As a Daddy Dom, Jax had a protective streak a mile wide, and it could rear its head at unpredictable times.

When they were younger, he and Jax had butted heads on occasion when Gavin felt the other man was overstepping his bounds, insulted Jax had thought it necessary. Looking back, Gavin wondered how differently his life would have gone if he'd heeded some of Jax's advice and warnings.

"I was, but I decided her need to run was actually a good thing."

"It is?" Aiden wrinkled his forehead in confusion. "Usually, when a woman runs away from me, that's a sign I need to let her keep on running." His expression changed, eyes refocusing, and he grinned. "Unless we're doing capture games. Then I'm supposed to run after her."

Ha. Gavin wouldn't mind doing some capture games with Leah. They'd make a mighty metaphor for their current situation. Chase after her, and when he caught up to her, toss her over his shoulder and... and hope he didn't throw his back out. Still, it could be fun if not quite the same as it had been before.

"If I hadn't gotten under her skin, she wouldn't have run. Running means she needs some time to think, and she doesn't think she can do it when she's next to me. So, she's not indifferent to me, and I'm making progress. She never felt the need to run after any of our scenes, but last night was different, which meant this morning was different."

"Do you think it was wise to let her go?" Aiden looked a bit skeptical. Both Jax and Gavin snorted. As difficult as Gavin and Leah's relationship had been over the years, when he compared himself to Aiden, he usually felt a little better about himself.

"What else was I supposed to do? Tie her to my bed and keep her there until it was time to go to therapy?" Truthfully, if he thought it would work... Leah would have eviscerated him when she got free.

Aiden shrugged.

"Or fuck her until she didn't feel like leaving."

As if it would be that easy. If Leah had stayed around for more sex, Gavin would have been *more* concerned, she didn't care.

"You have a lot to learn about women, my friend," Jax said, chuckling. He glanced at his watch and started putting things away. "And on that note, I need to get going."

"I know plenty about women." Aiden mock-scowled as Jax got to his feet, picking up the empty containers his food had been in. He winked. "I've been married twice."

Snorting with laughter, Jax shook his head and threw his containers away before saying his goodbyes, leaving Gavin to Aiden's tender mercies. It wasn't all that uncommon lately, to be truthful. Other than game night, Jax hadn't been around much.

"Have you seen much of Jax lately?" he asked Aiden as they decamped to the living room to let their stomachs settle before heading to the gym.

Aiden shook his head, settling on the couch.

"He's been busy with Esther and the kids. Something about softball season?"

"Ah, right." Gavin nodded. He remembered those days. When Mitch had been doing sports, his games were usually on Saturdays, not Sundays. That's why they'd set their gym date for Sundays in the first place. Maybe they should ask Jax if there was a better day for him. "Well, his loss."

"His gain, if we're talking weight," Aiden murmured, and Gavin chuckled, settling down on the couch beside him. It might not be the way he wished he was spending his Sunday morning, but it sure as hell beat sitting around on his own. He hoped Leah was having a better time of it.

CHAPTER FOURTEEN

LEAH

Dr. Silverwood wasn't anything like what Leah had pictured, although she hadn't quite known what to expect—a sweet, older woman who Gavin could push around, maybe, or a younger woman who was easily dazzled by Gavin and maybe even had a bit of a crush.

Instead, Dr. Silverwood was a no-nonsense woman who gave off a similar energy to Cyana. She was perfectly poised and very much in charge of the room from the moment Gavin and Leah entered, and she had a very calming presence. Silvery blonde hair, similar to Leah's, was cropped short at her chin in a classic bob, and she wore silver-rimmed glasses, a beige pantsuit, and chunky silver jewelry. Her smile was small but present, and she regarded Leah warmly, which was something Leah had been a bit nervous about, considering she didn't know what Gavin had said about her.

He said he wanted to get back together with her, so she supposed whatever he'd told Dr. Silverwood couldn't be *too* bad, but…

"Welcome, Leah, I'm glad you could join us today." Dr. Silverwood shook Leah's hand before settling into the chair in front of her desk. She held a clipboard and pen in her hand, balancing them on top of her crossed legs when she set them down.

"Thank you," Leah said, but she didn't say she was glad to be there. She wasn't actually sure whether or not she was. Both Cyana and Esther had been encouraging after talking to Jax and Aiden, who both thought Gavin was in earnest and ready to make a real change.

At least Leah was comfortable. There was something very soothing about the room. The walls were painted sky blue, and the chair Dr. Silverwood was sitting in was a darker shade of blue that went well enough to be calming to her eye. There were two more armchairs made of the same fabric, as well as a matching couch. Dr. Silverwood could easily face either from her current position, but Gavin headed straight for the couch, leaving Leah wondering whether she should sit next to him or put some distance between them by choosing one of the armchairs.

After a moment of hesitation, she sat on the opposite end of the couch, the same piece of furniture, but still giving them some distance. When she peeked at Gavin, he was looking at her, and he smiled as if to say he knew what she was thinking. Leah pursed her lips and looked back at Dr. Silverwood, who was watching them with a neutral expression.

Leah wondered what their little interaction had indicated to the psychologist. Was she thinking Leah sitting on the couch instead of farther away in the chairs meant she was interested in getting back together with Gavin?

Shit. Did her choosing the couch mean something?

Argh. Why was this so scary? She needed to get her shit together.

"So, Leah, we can start with you if you'd like to tell me a bit about yourself, or if you want some time to get comfortable, I can start with Gavin." Dr. Silverwood's eyes were dark brown and as penetrating as any Dominant at Outlands. She was a scary lady, without even trying, yet Leah felt comfortable with her, maybe because she was used to hanging around Cyana. Possibly.

Part of her wanted to start airing her grievances immediately, so Gavin could really understand what he was up against, but curiosity propelled her to see what he had to say first.

"Can you start with Gavin?" Even though Dr. Silverwood had

offered, Leah couldn't keep the note of uncertainty out of her voice. The therapist studied her for a moment, making Leah want to shift uncomfortably in her seat, wondering what Dr. Silverwood thought about her request, before turning her attention to Gavin.

Of course, Gavin was completely unperturbed by the woman's sharp focus. He even looked relaxed, with his hands on his thighs and a small smile as if he was perfectly happy to be there.

Of course, he is, now that it was his *decision to come here when he wouldn't before.*

"So, Gavin, how has your week gone?" Dr. Silverwood asked.

GAVIN

As much as he wanted to know what Leah had to say, he supposed it was only fair she got a chance to acclimate and see how open he was willing to be during this session. Not knowing whether he'd get the chance to have Leah come with him again, he intended on being as open as possible. This might be his biggest chance to really demonstrate how serious he was about making things work with her again.

Considering how much time had gone by, he didn't think it was going to happen unless he was willing to give it his all, so that's what he meant to do.

"Good. No, great," he corrected himself, turning his head slightly to flash a smile at Leah. "I was thrilled Leah gave me the opportunity to convince her to come with me today." Leah's eyes narrowed dangerously. Yeah, he doubted that was how she'd put it, but that *was* how he saw it. "I've been working on being more open with my feelings and communication. On Sunday, two of my friends came over for a bit. They wanted to know what was going on with Leah and me, and I told them."

"How did you convince Leah to come in today? Last week, you didn't seem hopeful it would happen any time soon." Dr. Silverwood studied him intently. For all intents and purposes, they were acting as if Leah wasn't there, which made it a bit easier on him. He'd gotten used to sharing with Dr. Silverwood but being vulnerable with the person who could actually hurt him... that was harder.

He also didn't want to inadvertently embarrass her. Slanting a glance Leah's way, he waited for her nod before he filled Dr. Silverwood in on their weekend activities. Since he wasn't facing her, it was hard to tell Leah's reaction to his recitation, but he saw her shifting in her seat a few times as she listened.

Surprised by how much he was willing to share?

Embarrassed?

Hopefully, he'd find out soon.

"I really wasn't expecting her to be willing to come in so soon, but just like when she showed up at the club, I wasn't going to waste the opportunity."

"What opportunity were you grabbing by scening with her at the club?"

As always, Dr. Silverwood went straight for the throat, which was actually one of the things he liked best about her. She didn't skirt around the issues or let him slide with brush-off answers but went right to the heart of matters. For someone who had trouble expressing himself, it was uncomfortable but a relief.

"I saw the opportunity to keep her tied to me," he said honestly. Out of the corner of his eye, he saw Leah jerk in reaction. He turned his head slightly, giving her a rueful, almost apologetic smile. "I know she won't go looking for other men if she's sleeping with me, which cuts down on my competition. I want her whole focus."

Leah appeared shocked, but he couldn't tell if she was shocked by how manipulative he'd been or because he'd admitted it. Hell, she might as well know if she hadn't figured it out already.

"And if she *did* date other men while you two are still scening together?" Dr. Silverwood drew his attention back to her. Jealousy roiled in his chest, and he rubbed his hand over the spot that tightened as if he could loosen it with his fingers.

"I wouldn't like it, but I'd deal with it and hope she didn't want to do so for very long." His smile was wry now. "I'd like to be exclusive with her, but that's what I want. I don't know yet what she wants."

LEAH

What do I want?

The answer to that question felt further away than ever. She was caught somewhere between yearning and resentment, hope and fury. The amount of anger bubbling up inside her was shocking. She'd thought herself over it. She'd thought she'd moved past it, but being here in Dr. Silverwood's office, listening to Gavin talking the way she'd wanted him to *years* ago was bringing up all sorts of emotions she'd thought were buried. Emotions that had raged after the divorce and before they'd managed to settle into their new routine, where she expected nothing from him, and they only saw each other for game night and kinky sex.

Yet she still melted at what he was saying.

Her emotions were like a yo-yo, yanking her back and forth and making her feel more vulnerable than ever, even though she hadn't said a word yet.

"What about you, Leah?" Dr. Silverwood asked. Leah froze, thinking the doctor was asking what Leah wanted before she went on. "How was your week?"

"Confusing." The word popped out of her mouth, a gut reaction. She could see Gavin frown and averted her eyes, focusing on Dr. Silverwood. It was so much easier to focus on the therapist than look at him. Her emotions didn't go quite so haywire when she couldn't see more of him than a fuzzy shape out of the corner of her eye. Pressing her lips tightly together, she found herself clenching her jaw. Now that they were here, it was surprisingly difficult to talk, despite Gavin going first.

"Was there anything in particular that confused you, or you'd like Gavin to clear up for you?" Dr. Silverwood made a small gesture above the clipboard on her lap—which she hadn't written on once so far.

"Not that he can clear up. He's made himself perfectly plain." Leah's jaw clenched again.

One of Dr. Silverwood's brows arched upward, questioningly, but she patiently waited for Leah to continue. If this lady wasn't a Domme, Leah would eat her hat. And if she wasn't, she easily could be if she wanted to. The single subs at the club who liked women would be crawling at her feet in much the same way they did for Cyana.

"I guess it's my own emotions that are confused. I know I should be grateful Gavin wants to do counseling…"

"Should you?" Dr. Silverwood asked when Leah's voice trailed off. Her brow had lowered, but she was still treating Leah to her particularly penetrating gaze. "Instead of talking about how you *think* you should feel, let's talk about how you actually feel."

"Confused. Again." Leah laughed, but it was a bitter sound. "Because part of me is grateful. Hopeful. I feel like I'm getting everything I ever wanted. But it's years too late." She waved her hand, and out of the corner of her eye, she could see Gavin flinch. "This is what I wanted a decade ago. Not now."

"If you don't want it now, why did you agree to come in today?" Dr. Silverwood asked. There was no judgment in her tone, only curiosity. Gavin, on the other end of the couch, was stiff and silent. Leah sighed.

"I guess because there is a part of me that does want it, but I'm afraid of getting hurt again."

"Understandably." Dr. Silverwood nodded. "You also seem a little resentful."

A bitter laugh bubbled up again, and Leah didn't like hearing it. She noted Gavin's wince with some satisfaction. It appeared he didn't like hearing it, either. Well, good. He should know she was ticked at him. In the past, she'd often hid her frustrations from him, not wanting to rock the boat, but now…

Fuck it.

"Resentful. Yes. Because once again Gavin is getting what *he* wants."

"I didn't want a divorce," he said quietly. Leah made herself turn to look at him again. There was enough pain in his eyes, in his expression, to touch even her heart, and she tried to harden it against him. "I tried to give you what you said you wanted."

"No, you didn't want a divorce, you wanted to go to couples therapy. Except I had already asked you to go to therapy with me months before that, multiple times, and every time, you turned me down. It wasn't until it was on *your* terms, you were willing to go." She pursed her lips and waved her hand again. "And here we are. On *your* terms."

"I'm sorry, love." His smile was weak. "Trust me, I wish I could go back and do it all over again... listened to you sooner."

The air rushed out of Leah's lungs, along with a lot of the bitterness. Hearing him say that soothed a lot of the anger churning inside her. Mostly because she knew there was no point to it. It's not like they *could* go back and do it all over again. They could only go on from here.

"Me, too," she said, but she said it softly, without any rancor, without the bitterness that had tinged her previous statements. She closed her eyes, turning her head to face front again as she took a deep breath.

Something touched her fingers, and she looked down, just then realizing she'd placed her hand on the couch beside her. It was on the center cushion, closer to her side than Gavin's. He had reached out to touch his fingertips to hers. Not holding them, not trying to grasp them... just touching them, tip to tip.

She looked up at him.

"Just the tip," he whispered, and she burst out laughing. Without the bitterness, without the anger, pure laughter that carried so much of her stress away. It wasn't even that funny, but Gavin was grinning and laughing, and Leah couldn't stop giggling. Even when she managed to tamp it down, little hysterical giggles kept escaping. It felt like forever ago they'd watched *Archer* together. She'd already been frustrated with him at the time, but she'd loved watching the show with him. It had appealed to both of their slightly fucked-up senses of humor.

"Well, I think this was a good start," Dr. Silverwood said, her lips very slightly curved into a small smile. "Same time next week?"

CHAPTER FIFTEEN

GAVIN

"The street is bustling, filled with people and stalls for shopping. A dog sits beside one of the food stalls. Colorful birds chirp from cages hanging from another stall. There are weapons, clothing, supplies for travel, and religious artifacts. It's loud, and the sellers are doing their best to engage your attention—"

"Is the dog for sale?" Aiden interrupted Gavin's long description of the street fair inside Alderic.

"No." Gavin opened his mouth to continue his description, but it was too late.

"Does he belong to the food stall owner?" Esther wanted to know, looking curious. Gavin sighed inwardly. Trust Aiden to get distracted and drag the rest of the group off course.

"No, he's just a stray dog." Unfortunately, before Gavin could yank them back on task, Aiden jumped in again.

"I want to feed the dog."

"What?" Gavin stared at him. He didn't have anything planned for the dog. It was just there to create ambiance. Which, of course, meant Aiden decided to focus on it.

"I want to feed the dog," Aiden insisted. "I want to try to make friends with it. You said he's a stray, right?"

"Yes, the fictional dog is a stray." Gavin now wished he'd said otherwise. Dammit. He glanced over to see Leah's reaction. She was grinning widely, gaze jumping back and forth between him and Aiden, clearly enjoying Aiden twitting him. Well, as long as he was making Leah smile, he'd take it—even if he wanted to smack Aiden on the back of his thick noggin. Cyana looked impatient as well, but she didn't say anything.

"Okay, then I want to make friends with the stray."

"Yay!" Esther clapped her hands before quickly sobering to the more serious demeanor of her elfin character. "I mean, good luck." Beside her, Jax chuckled and reached out under the table to hold her hand. Gavin wished he could do that with Leah, but as the Dungeon Master, he was—by necessity—too far away. Not that he'd be willing to relinquish his role, he liked being the Dungeon Master, even when his friends were doing their best to mess up his scenarios.

"Fine. Roll for Animal Handling," he said wearily, already going through the options in his head as Aiden picked up his die. Animal Handlings wasn't perfect, but it was the first thing he thought of, and he didn't think there were any rules for trying to make an NPC a pet. They were called Non-Player Characters for a reason. Under five and Aiden's barbarian was going to get his hand bitten. Maybe infected. Five to ten and—

"Nat twenty." Aiden grinned widely.

"What?" Gavin half-rose in his seat to try to see. *Goddammit.* The twenty was facing up on the die, the highest possible number Aiden could have rolled, which guaranteed his success, according to their house rules. Figured. The 'natural' twenty didn't happen often, but Aiden had a knack for rolling them exactly when Gavin wished he wouldn't.

"Of course, you get a nat twenty when it's something that doesn't matter and not when we needed you to get information out of that sorceress," Cyana muttered balefully, glaring at Aiden.

"It absolutely matters." Aiden eyed his dice. "Maybe I'm lucky right now… I should try some seduction on Ysolde over here…"

"You wish that was an option, and your 'persuasion' sucks, thank God," Cyana retorted. "You couldn't even persuade Ysolde to give you a hug."

"Maybe you could finish making friends with the dog," Leah pointed out, still grinning before Aiden could respond to Cyana, which was a good thing. She was getting that purse-lipped expression that said she was about two seconds away from physically launching herself at Aiden and smacking the back of his head.

"Right, right." Aiden's voice changed, deepening to the one he used for Morag. "Hey, there, little buddy, who's a good boy. You want to come travel with us?"

Gavin sighed again, but he couldn't stop the smile from curving his lips. This was why he loved this game—literally, anything could happen. He still remembered in the eighties when some people thought it was basically a Satanic cult and the Castle Masters were the priests who were leading the players down to hell and forcing them to do whatever the Castle Master wanted.

If only they knew. It was like trying to control chaos or herding unruly cats.

"I'm going to give the dog a piece of bacon," Leah said, her eyes alight. "I want to make friends with him, too."

Yeah, he had a feeling it was going to be a bit before he managed to get everyone back on track.

Leah

The guys ended up out on the balcony again during their break, giving Leah time to hang out with Esther and Cyana inside. Things didn't always split down the middle of the sexes during their breaks, but she knew Esther and Cyana wanted more than her text message that said the therapy appointment had been 'fine.' She'd pretty much been expecting the ambush tonight.

"Okay, quickly while they're outside... tell us everything," Cyana ordered, one eye on the guys as she leaned on Gavin's island's counter before taking a sip of the half-empty beer in her hand.

"It was... fine. Gavin updated Dr. Silverwood on everything that happened during the past week and our weekend. I got to talk a little about why I was ticked we were going to therapy now, on his terms, rather than back when *I* wanted to go."

Esther nodded thoughtfully, a small frown forming on her face. "What did he have to say about that?"

"He apologized. It was a good apology." Leah sighed, rubbing her hands over her face and glancing over at the balcony. She couldn't hear what the guys were saying, but Gavin and Jax were both laughing, probably at something Aiden said. "I don't know. I know we can't do it over, but... I don't know if I can move past it. It's not that I don't want to give him another chance, but a lot of resentment bubbles up every time I think about how much time has passed."

"Or you could think about it as, why waste any more time?" As usual, Esther had the sunnier outlook. "I mean, I get it. I've been resentful of Jax being so busy lately, but I can either let that go, so we can enjoy our time together, or I can simmer in it. I'd rather enjoy the time we do have together, even if I get ticked that he'd rather go to the gym with the guys on Sunday than hang out with me all day, even though he's been working extra hours. But I still got him Sunday night. I know it's not the same, but..."

"No, I get what you're saying." And it did make sense. It was just hard to get her emotions in line with the logic. They didn't necessarily want to cooperate.

"It does sound like he's trying," Cyana said, her tone more cautious than Esther's. "I have to admit, he's impressing me."

And considering how protective Cyana was—she'd been the one to give Gavin a come-to-Jesus talk about respecting Leah's decision at the end of their marriage—that was saying a lot. While she'd maintained friendships with both of them, she'd always made it clear she wasn't going to let Gavin steamroll Leah. Sometimes, Leah wished she didn't feel quite so much like a doormat in need of protection, although she also had to admit she'd needed Cyana to be the ball-buster at times when she'd been feeling especially weak.

Her friends balanced her out, Esther with her sunny optimism, and Cyana with her cynical protectiveness. Esther tried to protect her, too, but it was like the difference between a chihuahua and a mastiff. Esther just didn't have the same kind of intimidating vibe Cyana did.

"Here they come," Cyana said, straightening up. Leah turned to see Gavin smiling widely at her as he came back through the door. He winked. She flushed.

When the resentment wasn't holding her back, she could almost forget all the very good reasons she had for being unsure of him. Could she push it back all the time? Get past it enough to give them a real second chance?

Maybe Esther had it right. Maybe she needed to let go of her cynicism and see what Gavin was offering her now instead of focusing on the past.

GAVIN

When everyone else left, Leah went to use his bathroom, assuring Cyana she was fine and Gavin could walk her out if she needed it. Gavin's heart started to pound with hope. Leah never stayed behind. Even if she had, he would have expected her to ask Cyana to wait for her.

There was only one reason for her to stay behind tonight—she wanted to talk to him.

He'd thought the day had gone fairly well, though it had been hard to hear her resentment during the session with Dr. Silverwood. At least they'd ended on a good note. She had cause for resentment. It had stirred some of his own residual anger as well, but he'd pushed it back. He'd had weeks to work that out with Dr. Silverwood, whereas it had been the first time Leah was able to talk about it.

Keeping his cool was easier when he remembered how he'd ranted during those first few sessions with Dr. Silverwood.

Maybe he should see if Leah wanted to meet with the psych on her own to get some of that out where he didn't have to listen. He wanted to know how she was feeling, but he knew how therapeutic it was to be able to rant without having to worry about how the person listening would take his words. That was something they couldn't even get from their friends because there was no way for them to be unbiased.

The nerves started to get to him as he waited for her, so he tidied a few things up around the main areas of the condo. Okay, truthfully, he moved things around. Nothing really needed to be tidied. He cleaned up every Tuesday night in preparation for people coming over on Wednesday, which was how he kept the place neat, so there really wasn't much to do, but he found he couldn't sit still waiting for her.

When Leah came back down the hallway, she looked as nervous as he felt, which was some consolation. A small, unsure smile on her face, hands wiping damply at her jeans, she had worry in her eyes.

"Hey." He wasn't sure where to start.

"Hey."

Apparently, neither did she. But she was the one who had stayed behind. Honestly, he'd planned to give her some time, then try to contact her on Friday to see if she wanted to do something over the weekend. Try to make a date. So, he waited her out, wanting to know what she wanted to say rather than trying to take charge of the conversation like he normally would. It felt odd, but after a long moment, it actually worked.

"I uh... I was thinking... or I guess, wondering, what would a second chance look like to you?"

The hope that had bloomed in his chest burst wide open, and he couldn't stop himself from grinning, even when it made her scowl. *Tread lightly, tread lightly...* She was still skittish, and he didn't want to fuck this up. As much as he wanted to blurt out, it meant getting back together, staying together, and growing old—well, older—together, that wasn't the first step. That was the end goal. They still had to get there.

"I'd like to start by taking you out on a date," he said softly. "A real date, I hopefully won't ruin."

Humor curved her lips and glinted in her eyes. That was a good sign.

"What else? How do we go from this,"—she waved her hand back and forth between them—"to… wherever you want to go."

Ah, perhaps it *was* time to be clear.

"I want us to go back to being married, or if not married, then in a committed relationship and living together for the rest of our days. You in my arms every night and there beside me when I wake up in the morning. I'd prefer married; it makes all the legal stuff easier." He'd settle for her by his side because they could figure out the legal stuff. It would just take a little more work. She was worth the work. "I know it's not possible to start fresh or start over, but I'd like to start from where we are and rebuild what we had, but better this time because we know where we went wrong before."

"What about sex? The Outlands?"

Gavin spread his arms wide. He managed to keep his expression serious, but he knew his eyes were twinkling.

"Consider me at your service," he purred.

Leah gave him a look. "Be serious."

"I am, love. Any time you want sex or to scene, let me know." He'd pop a little blue pill if he had to, though he knew he didn't need his cock to satisfy her. Leah got satisfaction out of his pleasure, too, so he wouldn't want to deny her that.

"I don't know if I'm ready yet."

Dropping his arms to his sides, Gavin gave her his most disarming smile.

"Then that's fine too, love. We can take things slow." Whatever she needed. The physical part wasn't the problem for them.

"I don't know if I want *slow,* either." She scrubbed her hands over her face in frustration, and Gavin stepped forward, pulling her into his arms. To his relief, she snuggled against him, leaning into him for his strength, the way she used to.

"Lass, do you want me to make the decision?"

LEAH

Ugh. She shouldn't, right? That was one of their problems from before. Gavin had made so many unilateral decisions without ever consulting her, assuming he knew what was best. On the other hand, many times, she really had been relieved when he'd taken charge. It had been easier.

After all this time apart, she should know more of what she wanted. Right? She should be able to advocate for herself, but she *did* want someone else to decide. She wanted two things at once and didn't know what she wanted more. She wanted to keep her heart protected, but she didn't want to lose the connection they had now.

"That's wrong, isn't it? I should be able to decide. I shouldn't ask you to decide for me." Voicing the problem made her vulnerable, but Gavin didn't judge her. *Because he wants to make the decisions*, a cynical voice in her head pointed out. Leah decided to ignore it. She pressed her cheek against his chest, taking comfort in feeling his heartbeat and in the strong arms around her, holding her safe and secure.

Ironic, really, that the person who could hurt her the most was also the person who made her feel the safest.

"Remember what Dr. Silverwood said? Stop thinking about 'should' and focus on what you actually want. I have a suggestion if you want to hear it."

Well, that was new. She'd half-expected him to take over the way he would have in the past. Leah nodded her head, kinda wishing he wasn't wearing a shirt, so she could rub her cheek against the bristles of his chest hair. Why she'd always liked that feeling, she had no idea, but it was one of her favorites.

"Let's keep our relationship to the Outlands, for now. That way, we're keeping that part of our relationship at its current status rather than taking a step back. We can work on everything else. When we're ready, we'll move the sex either here or to your house."

"Here," Leah said immediately. Gavin chuckled, and she winced. She wanted it to be here because she was protecting her space, her home, just in case. She didn't want to go into this with him, already thinking it would fail, but she couldn't forget that was a possibility.

It was a good compromise. They could keep the good stuff in place and focus on what needed work. Talk. Date. She could do that. Leah relaxed. It helped that he'd asked if she wanted his suggestion. This wasn't giving way to him and what he wanted. It was talking things out as a couple. Progress.

"Here, at first. Hopefully, eventually at your place as well. Or our place. One step at a time."

One step at a time. She could do that.

Gavin's hand smoothed over her hair, and she felt his lips press against her forehead.

"Now, love, let me walk you to your car."

A little smile played on her lips. He'd often said much the same thing when they'd first started dating. Maybe they really could make this work better than before—they knew where they'd gone wrong the first time, and they had help. Yeah, she had some resentment to work out that they hadn't gone to therapy before, but Esther was right. She didn't want to waste any more time. They sure as hell weren't getting any younger.

CHAPTER SIXTEEN

GAVIN

His first date in forever. At least he'd been able to secure one. He'd even called up his son to get some ideas. It had been years since he and Leah had gone anywhere together, other than the Outlands, but Mitch knew all her favorite places. He'd thought about taking Leah back to some of their old favorites, but some of those were long gone, but he didn't want her to think he was trying to rehash their old relationship.

He wanted to build a new relationship on the foundation of the old one. That was how Dr. Silverwood had put it, and he liked that. It took into account the past, the present, and the future he wanted.

Instead of returning to one of their old haunts, they were going to the Pittsburgh Botanic Garden in Oakdale. Mitch said Leah loved it, and there would be a lot of flowers in bloom right now. Gavin had never been, and it wasn't somewhere he would have thought of taking her before, but if Leah loved it, he wanted to show her he'd be happy going anywhere with her, even places that didn't specifically interest him. He wanted *her* to be happy.

It was more than worth it, seeing the expression on her face when she realized where they were going. Her mouth actually dropped open in surprise as she straightened in the passenger seat.

"Seriously?"

"Seriously." Gavin grinned, enjoying the surprise and excitement he heard in her voice. Damn. Why hadn't he done more things like this when they were married?

Granted, they'd always felt it was important to do things separately as well as together, but they had so many things in common it made sense to do those things together. He should have done some of the things that only she liked to do some of the time. She'd gone golfing with him multiple times before he'd found out she didn't really like it, then she'd still gone a few times after that. Why hadn't he made an effort to return the favor?

Rebuilding. Don't look back, look forward, and do better.

No time for regrets, but he could certainly do better from here on out.

When they got out of the car, Gavin claimed Leah's hand. He'd warned her they'd be doing a fair amount of walking, but it would be relaxed, so she'd paired her comfortable sandals with a pretty short-sleeved dress covered in a riot of colorful flowers. It had a scooped neckline that didn't show a lick of cleavage, and the skirt came down to her knees, but she made it sexy.

"Are you sure you didn't know we were coming here?" he teased, nodding his head at the flowers on her dress. Leah laughed, her hand warm and resting easily in his. The sun shining brightly, brightening her blonde hair, made her appear almost ethereal for a moment.

"I would have *never* guessed," she said, shaking her head. Her grin was even wider than his, and Gavin's chest filled with pride at being able to both surprise and please her.

LEAH

She'd agreed to go on a date with Gavin, and she'd been a little excited about it—apprehensive as well—but she hadn't really expected it to be any different from the past. Her curiosity *had* been piqued when he'd told her to wear something for walking, but also that a dress would be fine. She'd thought maybe he was trying to throw her off and figured they were going bowling, to a game arcade, on a brewery tour, or something similar.

Things they'd enjoyed doing together in the past.

But the botanical gardens? Not where she'd pictured Gavin choosing to go. If she'd asked in the past, he would have turned her down, then she'd have come here with friends or her son instead. Hmmm. Speaking of which…

"Who did you ask for date ideas?" She was skeptical he'd come up with this one on his own but wanted to see if he'd reveal that.

"Mitch." Gavin squeezed her hand at her start of surprise. "He said you loved coming here. I figured we could look around, and you could show me your favorite part."

Well, color her surprised. He wasn't just bringing her somewhere unexpected, he was also letting her take control of part of the date. Curious to see exactly how far he'd go with this, Leah led him down the flower paths, telling him about some of her favorite flowers as they passed them—ones she had in her own garden, ones she wanted but didn't have space for—stopping to take pictures along the way. A few times, she stopped to read various signs along the way, just to see what Gavin would do.

To her bemusement, he seemed perfectly happy ambling along slowly, taking their time through the winding paths and listening to her ramble about plants. She knew he had no interest in gardening, plants, or flowers, but he listened and asked questions. Took pictures of her and didn't insist on being in them. Posed amiably when she said she wanted a picture of him in front of a bunch of pink azaleas.

Wearing a navy-blue shirt and jeans, surrounded by the bright pink flower bushes, he looked like he was modeling or something. The little half-smile on his face when she took his picture said he was enjoying himself.

If this had been a first date with someone she didn't have a past with, she would have called it her best first date ever.

The big jerk.

Then again, he had used insider information. Poor Simon hadn't had a chance by comparison.

"Let's get a picture together," Gavin suggested when they stopped on a bridge in the middle of the Asian Woodland section. The Lotus Pond was in full gorgeous bloom, and they were lucky enough there was a lull in other walkers. Gavin was already pulling out his phone, and Leah considered protesting for a moment, but...

If things do work out, I'll want this picture.

She stepped back against the railing but was surprised again when Gavin didn't go for the selfie. He wasn't really into pictures—Leah was always the one who suggested pictures and was usually the one taking them—so she'd figured he would do it quick and easy.

Instead, he let go of her hand and approached another couple a few feet down the bridge, who had also paused. The younger couple smiled and took his phone, and Gavin returned to her side.

"Who are you, and what have you done with my ex-husband?" she hissed at him, even more surprised when she didn't have to pose him. He pulled her in front of him and wrapped his arms around her, angling their bodies toward the young woman holding his phone.

"Think of me as Gavin 2.0, the upgraded edition," he murmured in her ear.

Leah giggled. The woman taking their picture smiled.

"Looks good! I took a couple, just in case," she said, holding out their phone to Gavin.

Another minute where Gavin took the young couple's picture in exchange, then he took Leah's hand again, and they kept walking. She couldn't deny there was a little pitter-patter going on in her heart that was completely unexpected.

Of course, her more cynical side reminded her, it wasn't the beginning of their relationship when things had fallen apart. It was once some time had passed, and he'd slowly stopped putting effort into it. Yeah, he was kicking things off in an amazing way, but it was the long haul that was really important.

Still, if this was an example of how he meant to improve on things, maybe she needed to stop being so cynical.

GAVIN

The morning at the Botanic Garden had been a major success. To his surprise, he hadn't been bored once. He might not care about flowers and plants, but he *did* care about seeing Leah enjoying herself, and that made all the difference. Her enthusiasm was infectious.

Afterward, they headed to the nearby strip mall for lunch.

"So, what do you think? Will I be able to convince you to go on a second date with me?" he asked, only a little nervous.

"I don't know, I guess it depends on where you want to go for date two," she teased, and he grinned.

"What if I want to surprise you again?"

Leah laughed, spinning her straw around her cup. "Honestly, I'm not sure you could surprise me much more than this. I do want to do things you're interested in, too. I know this morning wasn't really your thing."

"It was worth it to see how much you enjoyed yourself." Plus, being older and wiser, he'd enjoyed seeing the beauty of the gardens for what they were worth. Sometimes, it really did pay to stop and smell the roses. Especially when it made Leah smile at him the way she was right now.

"So, next weekend?" she asked.

"Sure, if you don't mind that it'll need to be either Sunday night or in the daytime." He supposed he could take a night off from the Outlands, but it made his skin itch to think about not being there on one of the busiest nights. Not that his presence really made that much of a difference, but it was a control thing. The Outlands was his, and he felt compelled to watch over them.

"You know that's fine with me." She pushed the ice around in her cup, dropping her gaze. "Do you... should we schedule a time to scene?"

Reaching out, Gavin placed his hand over hers, stilling her movements. When he touched her, she looked up at him again, and he could see the uncertainty in her eyes.

"Any time you want, love. Show up at the club, and I'm all yours." That left the ball in her court for sex, something else he wasn't used to. Of course, when she did appear, he'd take control, but letting her have complete control over the when was new to both of them. Gavin had enjoyed their impromptu scene last weekend, though he'd be better prepared for a spontaneous appearance in the future, even if that seemed like an oxymoron.

"I thought I might come by tonight," she confessed, her hand turning under his so their fingers could intertwine. Gavin smiled. "If that's okay."

"I said any time, and I meant it. I'm happy to schedule or play it by ear, depending on what you need."

"Then I'll be by tonight."

Their food arrived, and they let go of their hands. As they ate, he asked her how work was going, and they let the patter of regular conversation wash over them. Gavin had missed eating meals alone with her, where they could talk about everyday things. It was soothing to hear her stories from work, some of the names of her coworkers familiar, others totally new. She told him all about Oliver, and he was surprised at how much he enjoyed hearing stories of the kitten's antics.

Dropping her off at her home, he walked her to the door and dropped a hot and heavy kiss on her lips before taking his leave. Already, his head was spinning with ideas about what he could do with her tonight.

CHAPTER SEVENTEEN

LEAH

Walking into the club with Esther, Jax, and Cyana, Leah's nerves were ramped up higher than she'd anticipated. Maybe because, unlike last weekend, she'd come here deliberately to see Gavin and have a scene. Or maybe because, unlike last weekend, they'd already been to a therapy session and on a date. It felt as if the stakes were a little higher for the evening.

Jax and Esther walked in front of her, holding hands. Esther was bouncing with happiness about being there, the fluffy pink skirt she was wearing bouncing along with her. Seeing Esther's excitement, Leah was doubly glad she'd let her friends know she was going and asked if they wanted to come. Turning his head, Jax smiled down at his wife, and she beamed back up at him.

They really were too cute, and they needed this. She knew they hadn't been at the club in a while. Hopefully, they'd find some time to scene tonight.

Beside her, Cyana was on the prowl and even taller than usual in her six-inch heeled thigh-high boots. Leah had no idea how she managed to walk in those things. Back in their twenties, maybe even their early thirties, sure, but now? Leah's feet hurt just looking at them.

She'd opted for black sandals with a two-inch heel, which she could slip off easily enough before the scene started. While there were plenty of places to sit, on the weekends, it could get so crowded, seating outside of the aftercare section was at a premium, and she didn't want to risk having to stand for hours in shoes that hurt her feet.

Gavin would most likely be somewhere on the floor at this time of night, watching the various scenes, making sure everything was running smoothly. Thankfully, everything seemed to be going well, unlike the last time she was here.

Dressed in a navy-blue corset trimmed with black lace, nipping in her waist and pushing her boobs up into a shelf, it was a little hard to breathe, but she doubted she would be wearing it for long. The black faux leather skirt barely covered her ass and felt as if it was riding up with every step she took. Not that anyone here would care, but it was far from comfortable.

Absolutely worth it when she turned and met Gavin's eyes as he stared at her from across the room. People walked across his line of vision, but as soon as they were past, she could see his intense gaze still focused on her. Watching her. Eating her up with his eyes.

Arms crossed over his bare chest, she was pretty sure he was wearing his kilt, as usual.

"Go get your man, honey," Cyana said, and Leah jumped, squeaking when her friend's hand ricocheted off her ass. *Ouch.* Didn't matter that Cyana was half Gavin's size, she spanked just as hard.

Rubbing her butt, a smile curving her lips, Leah moved across the room toward her ex, her body already coming to life, humming with interest and anticipation. Didn't hurt she wasn't wearing underwear, which meant her folds were rubbing against each other as she moved.

Not enough to get her wet, but it still felt good. Tingly. *Arousing.*

"Good girl," Gavin said, reaching out to curve his fingers around the back of her neck and pulled her in for a seriously hot kiss. It was a sinful ravaging of her mouth, taking it for his own, demanding her submission.

Leah melted against him. The man knew how to kiss her to get her engine going. When he finally pulled away, his blue eyes were blazing with heat that washed over her like a warm ocean wave. All of her senses were humming with anticipation.

"Ready to play, love?" His finger stroked along the curve of her throat as if he was drawing a collar around it. Yearning slid through her.

"Yes, please, Sir." The 'Sir' tripped easily off her tongue, but there was a part of her that wanted to call him Master again. They weren't there yet, not for the collar or for the more intimate title. The fact she was even considering either was a huge step.

GAVIN

Leah's pretty bare throat bothered him in a way it hadn't in years, but there was nothing to be done about it. Part of their agreement after the divorce was she wouldn't wear a collar for him again. He didn't even want to think about how fast she'd slam the door shut on him if he asked her to put one on again, even in the club. Not even a 'just for the club' one.

Any collar would be a reminder of what they'd once had and how far they'd fallen.

If she ever wore his collar again, it would be because things progressed far beyond his wildest dreams. So, he could hold out hope, but not for any time soon.

Leading her to the St. Andrew's Cross he'd reserved for their use, he gave Tomas—the Dungeon Monitor standing guard over it—a grateful nod. Tomas had been keeping an eye on the stations around them but made sure the cross stayed unoccupied. Gavin hadn't known when Leah would arrive and wanted to make sure this particular one was available since it had a headrest. Grinning, Tomas gave him a salute before turning away.

"Shoes off, love," Gavin ordered, moving his fingers from the nape of her neck down to hold her hand, so she could steady herself against him while she took them off. Leah stepped out of the shoes, leaving her a couple inches shorter. "Hands behind your head."

Stripping her out of her corset and skirt was *his* pleasure and a good excuse to get his hands all over her lovely skin. His cock thickened as he got her naked and rubbed her all over. She sighed with relief when he pulled the corset off, leaving red imprints along her skin marked the boning pattern. She sighed again when he rubbed his hands over her ribcage and breasts. She'd once told him it made her tingle, and he liked the idea of being able to both soothe and arouse her simultaneously.

Her breasts were heavy in his hands, nipples already puckered in anticipation. Gavin gave them both a little pinch, making her squeak, and his cock jerked in response to the pretty sound.

"What's your safe word, love?"

"Hazard."

"Then let's get these pretty buds decorated, shall we?" He gave them another pinch, and Leah moaned, leaning into the pain, her eyes glazed from the pleasure. Tightening his grip on the tender nubbins, he watched as the pain flashed across her expression, a whimper working its way out of her throat as she went on her toes.

She didn't move her hands away from the back of her neck or try to pull away.

Gavin leaned over to brush his lips across hers.

"Such a good lass." He released his grip on her nipples, leaving her panting and his cock throbbing. Stepping away, he picked up the tweezer clamps from the station's table, where he'd laid them out in preparation. Since she'd given him the chance to prepare tonight, he knew what he wanted to do.

The three clamps were connected by chains, one of them dangling between the chain connecting the other two. Tweezer clamps were even less harsh than the ones he'd used last week because he was going for a more sensual scene tonight, and he didn't want her distracted from the flogging.

LEAH

Holding her position, breasts thrust out, legs spread shoulder-width apart, Leah shivered as Gavin attached the tweezer clamps to her nipples. The little buds throbbed pleasurably against the confinement, and her clit was throbbing even before Gavin knelt in front of her.

Gentle fingers parted her pussy lips, rubbing against her swollen clit, and she moaned, thrusting her hips forward. She wasn't very wet —apparently, they were going to need lube tonight—but damn, that felt good.

Not being as wet actually helped, allowing the rubber tips of the tweezer clamps to get a better grip on her pulsing clit. She shuddered as the tiny bud was pinched, her movement making her breasts bounce, which caused the chains to bounce, and the clamps tug on her nipples and her clit. All her most sensitive bits were throbbing.

Gavin jiggled the chain, and she gasped, the muscles all over her body tightening with the effort to hold still.

"Turn around and get up against the cross, love," Gavin said, getting to his feet and giving the side of her ass an affectionate slap. "Head against the rest but try to leave some space for the chains to dangle." Leah's pussy clenched, and she turned around as carefully as she could, but it didn't matter. Even the smallest movements made the chains tremble and tug at her nipples and clit.

She stretched her arms up, resting her forehead against the padded leather, leaning forward so her body wasn't against the cross and the chain connecting her clit clamp to the nipple clamp was unhindered. It hung between her and the padded rest her torso would have pressed against if she wasn't leaning forward.

Gavin came up next to her, and she closed her eyes, letting herself sink into an almost meditative state as he fastened leather cuffs around her wrists. Sighing happily, she let her muscles relax further, bracing herself against the cross with hands and forehead.

She didn't know what implement Gavin planned to use, but she was willing to bet a flogger. Her skin was already tingling in anticipation, her arousal curling higher as it wound its way through her senses.

Please, please, please...

"All set, love?"

"Yes, Sir." She sighed out the words. Fingers curved down her back to her bottom, giving it a squeeze before she heard him moving away again. Her skin felt warm where he'd touched her, a little tease of the heat she knew was coming.

The sounds of the club filled the space around them, adding to the atmosphere and the scene.

"Brace yourself, love." Gavin's voice came from a little farther away, low and serious. Leah kept her muscles relaxed and closed her eyes as she waited for the first impact.

Leather strands thudded down on her upper back and along her shoulders, like a painful caress, before falling away and returning to travel over her ass. Leah moaned and pushed her ass out farther, her movement setting the chains and clamps to pulling and tugging. She loved a nice thuddy flogger like the one Gavin was using, more sensual than painful, with just the right amount of bite.

Heat sank into her, enveloping her in a warm cloud, and she sighed with happiness. The rhythmic patter of the flogger against her skin was almost hypnotic, and pleasure coiled inside her in response. It was easy to lose track of time as her world narrowed to one of pure sensation.

Even if her eyes were open, she wouldn't be able to see anything in front of her. She couldn't move, thanks to the restraints around her wrists. Her own pants and moans were louder to her than the rest of the noise from the club, all of which melded together into an erotic white noise backdrop to the sounds she was making.

The flogger kissed her skin, over and over again, and her growing need made her squirm and wriggle under its lash. Her movements set off the chains and clamps, which tugged and pulled, sometimes gently, sometimes sharply, and always, always teasing. The one on her clit was becoming increasingly uncomfortable yet increasingly pleasurable as the little bud swelled against its pinching grip.

She might work herself up to orgasm from nothing more.

CHAPTER EIGHTEEN

GAVIN

Watching Leah carefully, Gavin could tell she was getting close to climax as the clamp on her clit did its work. She was squirming more, and it wasn't the flogger, but because of the sensations she was creating on her own. Her upper back and shoulders and the swells of her arse were a pretty shade of dark pink from the flogger.

Putting down the flogger, Gavin quickly removed his kilt and slicked some lube over his cock. Leah didn't even seem aware the flogging had stopped, which told him just how lost she was in the sensations.

Despite this being their second public sex scene in the Outlands, there were murmurs from their audience—some still in surprise, others in satisfaction. Gavin grinned. He'd always been a bit of an exhibitionist. There was something primal about taking his woman in front of people, unmistakably claiming her as his own.

Mine. Don't touch.

Fisting his cock in his lube-slicked fingers, he felt his own anticipation surge, the thick length hardening further in his hand. When he got behind Leah, he rubbed his fingers over her pussy lips, adding to the wetness already there. He could hear her whimpers, but when he touched her, she moaned, pushing her hips back at him. Giving the chains to her wrist restraints a quick adjustment, Gavin stepped behind her and curled his fingers around her hips, pulling her back toward him.

The chains lengthened, so she was bent over even more, her head now resting against the padding where her stomach would have been. Lining up his cock with her pussy, he thrust forward, burying half his cock inside her. Leah cried out as he filled her, the silken heat of her pussy gripping the length of his shaft. She was hot and swollen around him, her muscles clenching and pulsing, massaging him.

Keeping a firm grip on her hips, he pulled back out and thrust, deeper this time, burying himself in her slick channel. Leah's muscles shuddered around him, spasming pleasurably as they moaned in unison. He slapped her ass, making her clench around him, her pussy squeezing his cock in a tight vise of ecstasy.

"Yes, love, just like that." He spanked her again, plowing into her from behind with the vigor of his much younger self. Tomorrow his muscles might regret it, but right now, all he cared about was Leah's sweet cunt wrapped around his cock and the tremors of her body as she neared orgasm.

Leah

The sharp swats against her ass added another element of pain to the overwhelming sensual bliss Gavin had dropped her into. Moaning, writhing, Leah hung from her restraints, her legs trembling with the effort of keeping herself up. Thankfully, Gavin's hand on her hip gave her extra support, as did his thrusting cock. She was pinned in place between him and the cross, her breasts and chain bouncing and jiggling beneath her.

The sensitive nub of her clit throbbed harder than ever as if it was trying to burst out of the clamp, but there was no escaping its painful grip. The sensations collided, sparking off each other and creating tiny explosions as the air seemed to shimmer around her.

"Gavin!" His name fell from her lips as her entire body clenched and released, ecstasy streaming through her.

He moved harder, faster, approaching his own orgasm as she sobbed with the intense pleasure of her own. The rapture rolled on and on, pouring through her, consuming her. Every tug of the clamps on her nipples and clit sent another paroxysm of pleasure surging along her nerves until the ecstasy from each climax blended together, and she couldn't tell where one ended and the next began.

Gavin finally buried himself inside her, his cock pulsing against the squeezing walls of her pussy and flooded her with his own release.

Sagging, Leah could barely keep herself up. She heard Gavin bark some orders, but the words didn't come together to make sense in her head. A moment later, there were extra pairs of hands helping her stay upright as the leather cuffs around her wrists were removed, then she found herself wrapped up in a blanket and carried off to the aftercare area.

Not by Gavin, she realized when she was passed off onto his lap. Sleepily, she nuzzled into him, giggling a little at the idea that she'd been passed around like a happy little orgasm-drunk parcel.

"What is so funny, *mo chridhe?*"

"Me." She giggled again, feeling more than hearing his chuckle rumbling through his chest.

Everything felt wonderful, and she was also having trouble keeping her eyes open. Each blink felt heavier than the last until her lids went down and stayed there. Sighing, Leah gave herself over to the orgasm-induced exhaustion, knowing Gavin would keep her safe.

GAVIN

Hand stroking up and down Leah's blanket-covered body, Gavin observed the club around them. His body ached a little. The chair he'd used last week had been a lot kinder to his body than the standing position tonight.

143

Hopefully, he'd be able to convince Leah to come home with him sometime and do a scene there. He loved the club, and scening here fed his exhibitionist side, he would certainly enjoy having a bed—both to use during the scene and to collapse onto afterward.

There was no shame needing help to pick up Leah and get her over to the aftercare station after the scene. In her current state, she was basically dead weight. Still, it was a reminder he was getting older. Lowering his lips to her head, he gave her temple a gentle kiss.

This was the older he wanted—Leah cradled in his arms, both of them cuddled together—but he wanted to go home to the same house after and wake up in the same bed. Spend their evenings together and when they eventually both retired, spend their days together. Leah *was* his retirement plan.

That was still years off for her. He could probably sell the Outlands any time. He doubted he would do so until she retired. Though he could start practicing by not having to be here *all* the time, especially on the weekends. Compromise. Before, he'd expected Leah would understand he needed to be here, and she had.

Tonight, for the first time, he wished he wasn't here, which was unexpected. He'd assumed eventually, he'd start releasing the club's reins a little, but he hadn't thought it would be any time soon. It would be an adjustment but a worthwhile one. Leah would know and understand what a big step it was for him and how much it meant.

Who knew that he'd get better at bending as he aged rather than more inflexible? Funny how that happened. Not that Leah had changed him or even that her absence in his life had changed him, he wouldn't put that onus on her, but the lack of her in his life, in the way he wanted, had made him want to change.

"Aw, aren't you two cute?" Cyana came to a stop in front of him with Mistress Amara by her side, both of them grinning down at them. Amara was several inches taller than Cyana, her skin several shades darker, with very short hair shaved almost to the skin on the sides with short-cropped curls on top of her head. "How are your knees feeling?"

"A little creaky," he admitted, making them laugh. Leah shifted in his arms at the sound but quickly settled back down. "What can I do for ye?"

He knew they wouldn't have interrupted his aftercare time with Leah if they hadn't wanted something from him. The two exchanged glances before returning their focus to him, apologetic expressions on their faces.

"Alex is ready to sign a club contract with Paul but wants someone to go over it with him." Cyana said 'someone,' but they all knew she meant Gavin, who never let anyone else go over club contracts with submissives who requested help. He wanted to make personally sure they were advocated for.

Mistress Amara was good friends with Alex. She had been the one to sponsor him to the club and was very protective. He'd been skittish when first joining the club since he hadn't been 'out' publicly, in addition to being new to kink. That he was finally ready to sign a club contract was an amazing sign of progress.

Which was why she and Cyana came to help get Gavin. Pre-divorce, Gavin would have given Leah's aftercare over to a trusted friend, so he could take care of business. She said she understood, and he always came right back to her as soon as he could. It was something she hadn't brought up in any of their fights or during the divorce, but Gavin found himself reluctant to leave her, his arms tightening around her.

Well, he *had* just been thinking about giving over some control and responsibilities in the club. Did he really *need* to be the one to go over the contract with Alex? No. If anything, Amara would be even more aggressive, making sure Alex understood every part of it and agreed to all the terms because it was personal for her. Which wasn't any different from other times in the past when Gavin had insisted on being part of the process, but that was because he hated giving up control.

Especially when a club contract was being signed in *his* club.

Maybe this was what personal growth felt like—slightly painful but also a relief.

"Can you two take care of it?"

Mistress Amara blinked in obvious surprise while Cyana smiled approvingly.

"Of course, I can," Amara said. She glanced at Cyana. "We can." Since Cyana was not only Gavin's friend but one of the Dungeon Monitors, she'd be a good stand-in for him.

There was an odd tightness in his chest, and he felt a little antsy at the thought of not being part of the process, but he also felt he was right where he was supposed to be right now. Who knew how long Leah would be out of it. He wasn't leaving her side until she was more coherent, and it wasn't fair to make Alex and Paul wait since Gavin didn't know when he'd be available—or *if* he'd be available tonight.

"You can use my office. Leave a copy of the contract on my desk." He would look it over later. That was part of the reason he liked to be part of the process. He wanted to make sure he knew the terms of every club contract. So far, there had only been one incident, ever, where he'd had to step in because a Dom violated the terms of the contract, and the submissive had been too far gone into subspace to safe word, but even one was too many as far as Gavin was concerned.

Who would keep track of all the contracts and terms on nights when he didn't come into the Outlands?

Figure it out later. Baby steps. Start with this.

Amara nodded, straightening up and stalking off through the crowd.

Stepping forward, Cyana patted him on the shoulder.

"It's about time," she murmured before following after Amara. Good to know she approved.

Leaning back against the sofa, Gavin made himself relax. He couldn't be in two places at once, and he'd decided to put Leah first from here on out. This was proof he could do so. She was asleep, and he didn't plan on telling her since he didn't think he could do so without sounding awkward or pushy.

But *he* knew he'd done it.

CHAPTER NINETEEN

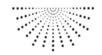

Leah

"Ms. Elliott? Ms. Elliot?"

Leah jerked to awareness. She hadn't even realized she'd been staring off into space. Standing in the doorway to her office, one of the junior associates was nervously shifting her feet. What was her name again? Teresa? That's right.

"Yes, sorry. I was... thinking," Leah said, clearing her throat and straightening up.

"The Boson account?" Teresa asked, bobbing her head sympathetically. Young but smart as a whip, Teresa needed self-confidence more than anything. She often showed up in Leah's office, wanting someone else to look over her work. Leah didn't mind, especially because she could see Teresa's confidence slowly growing as Leah encouraged her.

She tried to give off the image of a strong, confident, put-together woman, so it was a little disconcerting to realize she'd been daydreaming about her ex-husband instead of thinking about the upcoming presentation they had for the Boson account. Granted, it didn't help that her clit and nipples were still sensitive from Saturday night, though they were no longer sore. Thank goodness for padded bras since the merest touch was still making her nipples stand at attention.

"I have some ideas," Teresa said, stepping into the office and drawing Leah's focus back to where it was supposed to be. She shyly laid out the sketches she'd been holding. Leah leaned forward, tugging one of them in front of her.

"These are wonderful, Teresa!" Time to get her head back into the game.

Thirty minutes later, when Teresa left her office, glowing from the praise, Leah was sure they were on the right track for the Boson's marketing promotion. It was one of the biggest accounts, and she was sure they were going to be pleased. Teresa's suggestions managed to be fresh *and* on-brand, and Leah had shown her how to further fine-tune some of her ideas.

Leah was thankful she had such a good team around her because even knowing she needed to focus, she was still struggling. Not because of the sex or the lingering effects on her body, but because *she* was struggling with what she wanted. If she'd made a decision, it would be easier, but she hadn't.

She couldn't shake the feeling of waiting for the other shoe to drop.

Yes, everything with Gavin had been wonderful... so far.

Yes, Gavin seemed to have made some changes that would make their relationship better... so far.

Was she worried if she gave in, if she said 'yes, unequivocally yes,' all the effort he was putting in right now would stop?

Maybe.

Yes.

Argh. She *wanted* to be able to trust things would keep going the way they were... Maybe she was being too hard on herself. This was pretty new, and she and Gavin had only gone to one session with Dr. Silverwood together, although he'd been going on his own for months.

She should probably bring this up on Wednesday.

GAVIN

This week, Leah had chosen to sit in the center of Dr. Silverwood's couch rather than on the opposite side. Gavin felt as if that was a good sign. She wasn't leaning toward him or taking his hand, but still.

Baby steps.

It was also interesting hearing Dr. Silverwood talk to Leah about some of the things she brought up since they were things Gavin had felt but hadn't been able to verbalize, or if he had, he hadn't been able to do so in a way Leah understood what he was trying to say. Dr. Silverwood didn't have any of the emotional baggage from their relationship, so she could say it without putting Leah on the defensive.

"To me, when I asked Gavin to go to couples counseling before, it was a last-ditch effort to save our marriage," Leah said, rubbing one of her hands nervously against her thigh. He wasn't sure she even realized she was doing it. "When he said no, it felt like he didn't care about saving it at all."

Yeah, Leah might not be the only one who immediately bristled on the defensive. Gavin clenched his jaw, stifling his kneejerk reaction to ask how she could possibly say that. It didn't fit with how he'd felt at *all*, but he knew this wasn't about him, wasn't about how he'd felt, but acknowledging how she'd felt.

"Gavin, did you realize it was a last attempt to save the marriage?" Dr. Silverwood asked him directly.

"No. I didn't realize we needed saving at that point. I mean, I wouldn't say everything was going great, but I didn't think we were headed toward divorce." He rolled his head around on his neck, trying to loosen the muscles there. "I didn't see the point of counseling. No offense, doc. I mean, I thought we were doing okay, maybe stuck in a rut, but I didn't think we needed outside help. I didn't want anyone butting into our relationship."

"Did you ask Leah why she was interested in counseling?"

He tipped his head back, trying to remember. At the time, he'd been focused on keeping the Outlands running and in the black, being on point as Dungeon Master for their weekly game, so he didn't disappoint anyone, worrying over whether or not he was giving Mitch good advice about puberty and women, and Leah had taken a bit of a back seat when it came to his priorities. A sobering realization.

"No. She didn't really push it, so I figured it wasn't that important to her." Gavin sighed. "I probably should have asked her why she wanted to go."

"Do you remember what your response was to her?"

Gavin shook his head.

"I do." Leah's tone was a little tart, and she stared straight at Dr. Silverwood rather than looking at him. "He said we were fine, so we didn't need counseling. Except we weren't fine, clearly, which was why I was asking for counseling."

His shoulders sagged. Dammit. Why hadn't he asked her? Yeah, he'd assumed they were fine, but she had a point. What had he been thinking? That they didn't have the time, probably, or they could work things out on their own. She'd been unhappy enough to feel as if it was a last-ditch attempt at making their relationship work, and he hadn't even known.

Hindsight was twenty-twenty.

To his surprise, Dr. Silverwood didn't immediately agree with Leah.

"It was clear to you, but did you tell Gavin why you wanted counseling? Do you think it was clear to him?" There was no judgment in Dr. Silverwood's voice, but Gavin could feel Leah bristle next to him, much the same way he had a moment ago. Just like him, she didn't let her temper get to her. There really was something to be said for having an unbiased, uninvolved third party listening and responding to their complaints.

"I… I mean, why else would I have asked for counseling?"

LEAH

Even asking, Leah cringed because she knew she was avoiding the question.

The answer was no, she hadn't told him she wanted counseling because she felt like she was drowning in their marriage. She hadn't told him it was her last-ditch attempt to save them. She'd asked, he'd said he didn't think they needed it, and she'd taken it as him writing them off as a couple.

Even when she'd realized he'd been surprised how unhappy she was in their marriage, she'd taken it to mean *he* was the problem because he hadn't noticed how miserable she was. With Dr. Silverwood's cool eyes on her, Leah felt herself shrivel a little inside because it didn't seem like the doctor agreed. Worse, Leah could see the point.

"One problem that comes up often in my sessions with couples is different communication styles," Dr. Silverwood said, rather than answering Leah's question. Leah scrunched down in her seat. Part of her wanted to lean toward Gavin for reassurance, but she made herself stay put. Who knew if he'd be willing to offer any right now, after having it pointed out she'd basically expected him to read her mind? "Everyone has their own way of communicating, but a lot of it can be broken down into whether you're an 'ask' person or a 'guess' person."

Leah snuck a glance at Gavin. She was willing to bet he was an 'ask' person, and she was a 'guess' person. Her stomach did a little swooping dip. Being a 'guess' person didn't sound good.

"There's nothing wrong with either method." It was as if the doctor had heard Leah's thoughts. "But it can cause conflict. Askers tend to be direct about what they want, whereas guessers can find direct requests off-putting or even rude. What we need to do is find a way for you to both keep in mind how the other person communicates and make allowances."

"Like, I should have asked Leah why she wanted to go to counseling." There was a lot of resignation and self-recrimination in Gavin's voice, and Leah had to keep from reaching out with her hand to offer *him* comfort. She glanced over, and her heart melted when she saw the sad expression on his face. "I didn't realize there was a deeper meaning behind it, but I also didn't take the time to find out."

"Yes, exactly." Dr. Silverwood smiled at him, like a teacher pleased with her star student. "Leah, what do you think you could have done?"

"I could have told Gavin why I wanted to go." Even thinking about it made her stomach roil. "Or told him how upset I was when he said no."

"Both good answers."

"Is this because I'm submissive? Is that why I'm a guess person?"

To her surprise, Dr. Silverwood immediately shook her head.

"There are many submissives who instinctively ask for what they need and as many dominants who are more comfortable not asking when outside of a kink situation. This is not a one-size-fits-all personality trait."

Leah didn't know if that made her feel better or not. It sounded to her like being an 'ask' person was the better way to be, but she really did feel bad when she had to ask for something directly, as though she was making it hard for the other person to say 'no.' It wasn't as if she hid her intentions. A lot of what she wanted were normal things, things she really shouldn't have to ask for.

"Okay, but…" Leah blurted, then caught herself. Gavin and Dr. Silverwood looked at her, waiting, and she hesitated for only a moment before forging ahead again. She felt incredibly fidgety and uncomfortable, but she made herself spit it out. "It doesn't feel as if it's *real* if I ask him to do something. Like, I wouldn't ask him to buy me a gift. I want him to *want* to get me a gift."

"If you want a gift, of course, I want to get you a gift," Gavin said, a frown forming on his face. "Why would asking for it make it mean less?"

"Because you should get it because you're thinking of me, and you think I might want it, not because I asked for it." It didn't sound right when she said it out loud, but it felt right. Frustrated, Leah grit her teeth. "I wanted you to want to go to couples therapy with me, not go because I was forcing you."

"You wouldn't be forcing me if you asked, and I agreed to go. If I didn't want to go, I wouldn't go. I would know it was something you wanted to do."

"Yeah, well, I tried that when I asked you if you wanted to go to counseling, but it turned out you didn't want to go." Bitterness coated her voice so thick, she could practically choke on it.

"If I'd known how important it was to you, I would have in a heartbeat! Hell, I asked *you* to go once I realized you were going to leave me."

Yeah, but by then, it had been too late because she hadn't told him how important it was to her that he said yes, that he wanted to go to counseling, wanted to fix things. He hadn't known how unhappy she was because she hadn't told him but also because he hadn't noticed.

Because they sucked at communication.

Gavin cursed and reached out, hauling her onto his lap, and only then Leah realized tears were rolling down her cheeks. He'd done it without hesitation in the middle of them fighting—again—whereas she'd been too timid to reach out and take his hand a few minutes ago. Too afraid of making herself vulnerable to him. Why she hadn't asked for things she wanted—asking made her vulnerable. He might say no.

He also might say yes.

Crying harder, Leah clung to him, not caring if Dr. Silverwood was watching or what she thought.

It was my fault.

It was a hard admission to make to herself but an important one.

GAVIN

Holding Leah in his arms while she sobbed, Gavin felt even more helpless than usual. He didn't know how to fix this, didn't even know why she was crying. Well, he sorta knew why she was crying, but he definitely didn't know how to soothe a decade-old hurt. His own eyes stung with unshed tears that threatened to spill over, his heart aching like it was breaking all over again.

"This is all my fault," he muttered, squeezing her more tightly against him because it was the only thing he *could* do. Why hadn't he questioned her motives when she'd first suggested counseling? Pride? Lack of time? The arrogant assurance he didn't need to do anything more than he already was because she'd be there, regardless? He'd been an ass.

"No, this is my fault. I didn't even *try* to tell you... I was too afraid..." Leah hiccupped, cutting off her words, but Gavin understood.

"You shouldn't have had to tell me. I'm the 'asker.' I should have asked."

To his surprise, Leah giggled and hiccupped at the same time.

"It's not anyone's fault," Dr. Silverwood said smoothly, cutting back into the conversation. "It's a breakdown in communication, and there are things both of you can do to improve your communication with each other. I would rather see both of you focusing on what you want to do to improve rather than thinking about what you didn't do in the past."

Gavin and Leah looked at each other. Despite the tears in her eyes, Leah was smiling again.

"I think we can do that, doc," Gavin said, giving Leah a crooked smile of his own.

Dr. Silverwood was right. Assigning blame to the past didn't help anything, but now they could see the other person's perspective of those events. It was a little daunting, but not a bad thing.

"Yeah." Leah's smile was still a touch watery, but at least the flow of tears had stopped. "We can do that."

CHAPTER TWENTY

LEAH

Back at work after such an intense second session with Dr. Silverwood, Leah surprised herself by having no trouble focusing and being able to knock out some stellar ideas for the Boson account. Maybe some of the stuff that came out during the appointment had also jogged her creative side. Or maybe she was feeling better about her and Gavin in general, so she wasn't as distracted.

Either way, it was a productive afternoon.

Swinging by home to change her clothes and feed Oliver before she headed over to Gavin's for game night, she found herself picking out slightly sexier clothes than she might have a few weeks ago. Not for armor... she wanted to be attractive to him.

Which, considering how emotional their session had become, might not make sense to some people, but she actually felt closer to him than ever. They'd both had their faults, and now they could both see how they'd contributed to the situation. She still felt guilty for her part—especially for not recognizing the part she'd played—but she knew Gavin did as well. That put them on the same page about everything for the first time... and it felt good.

Brushing out her hair, she decided to leave it down. A quick touchup to her makeup. Adjust the 'girls,' so her cleavage looked good in the sky-blue shirt she was wearing. Ready to go.

"Bye-bye, cutie pie," she said to Oliver, giving him a little kiss and a stroke on his head. He opened his eyes but didn't deign to move. Now that he'd been fed, he was all sleepy and happy. "Be a good boy. I'll see you when I get back."

Humming happily all the way to Gavin's building, for the first time in a very long time, she showed up before everyone else. At least, she didn't see anyone else's car in the parking lot.

Heart thumping in her chest, she made her way to his door and let herself in. Since Aiden was in charge of dinner this week, she wasn't surprised to find Gavin sitting in the living room rather than in the kitchen. His head came up as she walked in the front door and the surprise on his face, followed by his appreciation as his eyes traveled over her body, was very welcome.

"I didna expect to see you here this early," he said, his brogue a little thicker than usual as he got to his feet, and Leah grinned.

"I was surprised I beat everyone," she confessed. She stood awkwardly as Gavin came toward her, unsure what to do. Normally, everyone greeted each other the same as everyone else did, hugged if it felt appropriate, but she had no idea what to do when it was just the two of them.

Thankfully, as usual, it seemed Gavin did. Cupping her face in his hands, he dropped a kiss on her lips, not long or deep, but a sweet kiss that made her insides fizz. He pulled away, but his hands remained where they were.

"Can I get ye a drink?"

"Water would be great." She smiled up at him. Considering how hungry she was, going straight for the wine probably wouldn't be the best idea.

Jax and Esther showed up while Gavin was getting her water, cutting off any chance for intimacy. Feeling a little disappointed, Leah chatted with them while they settled in on the couch. A few minutes after they arrived, Cyana came in before Aiden finally showed up, arms laden with several pizza boxes, about ten minutes late.

"It's about time," Cyana complained, jumping up to help him with the boxes.

"Well, I would have hurried if I knew you were so excited to see me, sunshine," Aiden replied, grinning and winking at her. Cyana rolled her eyes and didn't deign to reply.

"That smells amazing," Esther said, coming over to help arrange the boxes on Gavin's island while he passed out the plates.

It really did. Leah tried to eat pretty healthy the rest of the time but considered game night her cheat days, sometimes ending in heartburn, but it was worth it.

Something felt different about tonight. The camaraderie or... she wasn't sure, but when Gavin sidled up next to her, sliding his arm around her waist while they waited for their turn to pick up their slices, she didn't stiffen or pull away. It felt... right. Good.

She ignored the little sidelong looks their friends were giving each other.

***

GAVIN

"Okay, so I've created a chart for the dog." That damn dog, who still didn't have a name since no one could agree on one. Gavin had started calling it TDD in his head, short for 'that damn dog.' He'd needed a mechanic to figure out who the dog would listen to when given conflicting orders, and it made sense the dog was most loyal to whoever commanded it. There wasn't a whole lot of guidance on having a pet, so he was making it up as he went. The chart gave him a bit of structure.

"What kind of chart?" Cyana asked, frowning. Out of all of them, she'd been the least interested in the dog. She'd been amused by its presence and Aiden and Esther's attempts to slather affection on a fictional pet, but nothing more. Leah and Jax had both spent some time interacting with the dog, although not as much as Aiden's and Esther's characters.

"We'll call it a love chart. It'll help me keep track of how much loyalty the dog feels for each of you based on your interactions with it."

To his surprise, Cyana straightened up with interest.

"You'll know who the dog loves the best?"

Next to her, Aiden scowled and shot her a dark look.

"He already loves me the best. I'm the one that's been paying attention to him."

"Hey!" Esther protested from across the table. "I have been, too! He might love me the best!"

"*Stop it!*" Gavin roared before the conversation devolved into an argument over who the fictional dog loved the best. Mouth quirking with amusement, Jax reached over to put his hand on his wife's shoulder, but Esther shrugged him off, still glaring at Aiden. "I didn't have this chart before, so we're starting at a baseline out of ten. Right now, Xidria and Morag are the same are at a four. Then Leandrin at three, and Doklos at two. It has no interest in Ysolde." Naming off everyone's characters, based on who had shown the dog the most interest in the last game, Gavin glared at all of them.

Esther and Aiden looked pleased, although they were still giving each other dirty looks about their characters being tied. Jax was frowning, but it was impossible to tell if it was because Doklos was behind Leandrin or if he was annoyed Esther had shrugged him off.

Cyana looked ticked.

"I didn't know there was going to be levels," she muttered darkly before turning to look at Gavin, her chin tilting up. "I want to give the dog... a treat."

Gavin wanted to pound his head against the table because he'd somehow managed to make this a competition, and now even *Cyana* was going to be obsessed with the dog. Probably should have seen that coming, but it had annoyed him that Esther and Aiden had kept trying to get the dog to 'like' their characters without having any actual measure for how it was going.

Ah, the life of a Dungeon Master.

"Fine." He sighed. "Roll for Animal Handling."

Cyana tossed her dice into her tray and frowned.

"Shit. Two."

"Yeah, the dog just bit you."

LEAH

After one of the more entertaining—and utterly useless—evenings they'd had in a while, Leah lingered again, letting the others leave before her. She knew she couldn't stay, but she wanted that bit of alone time with Gavin before she left.

Closing the door behind Aiden, Gavin turned and raised his eyebrows.

"I dinna suppose I could talk ye into spending the night?" His voice had gone a little deeper, the question coming out as a seductive invitation, made all the more so by his deliberate leaning into his accent. Leah smiled ruefully at him. There was no expectation in his gaze. He didn't think she would say yes, yet he'd made the invitation all the same.

Asking.

Something she was going to try to be better at.

"Not tonight. Walk me to my car?" By now, the others would have already driven away, giving them at least a modicum of privacy. She wanted him to walk her to her car. Such a simple request, one she *knew* he would say yes to, yet she still felt oddly uncomfortable asking instead of waiting for him to *guess* that's what she was hoping for, the way she had last week, but she did it and oddly felt like cheering.

"Absolutely." He held out his arm, and Leah wrapped her hand around his elbow, stifling a giggle at his faux-courtly manners. "Can I take you out again this weekend?"

"I have some plans to work in my garden… want to come over and help with mulching?" Two asks in under five minutes. This one didn't feel as difficult, maybe because it wasn't something she cared too much about—and certainly not something she expected him to say yes to, though she would like it if he did.

"Sure, why not?"

"Really?" Part of her had thought he might say yes because he was trying to show her his best side, another part of her had assumed he would say no. He'd hated mulching when they were married, but he'd always come out to do it when he'd seen her out there.

It occurred to her she hadn't asked him to do so back then, but he had, anyway. He hadn't liked seeing her struggle. She'd always felt torn when he did because she liked having him out there with her but also felt guilty he was doing something she knew he didn't like doing. Now, looking back, she could see he'd done it for her. She shouldn't have felt guilty. It wasn't as if she'd forced him or even asked him.

Hmmm, maybe that was another reason she had trouble asking for what she wanted. She didn't like to be a burden to other people, especially not to her romantic partner. *Oi.* All sorts of revelations were coming out today.

"Yes, any excuse to spend time with you." He winked at her, and she found herself giggling and blushing. When he said it like that... "Besides, I had a good time at the Botanic Gardens with you. I like to see you enjoying yourself, and I know you enjoy gardening. Hell, now that I'm older, maybe I'll like it better."

"Which is why you moved into a condo, completely devoid of yard or plants?" Leah teased. They stopped at her car, Gavin tilting his head to the side as he considered her words.

"You know... I don't think I'd really thought about it like that when I bought this place, but yeah."

Leah laughed.

When Gavin pulled her into his arms, she ran her hands up his biceps, enjoying the feel of his muscles tensing beneath her fingers, his hard body supporting hers. It was a softer body than in their younger years, but that didn't bother her. A little more cuddle quotient never hurt anyone.

"Think you'll come by the club this weekend?" he asked, stroking hair back from her face.

"Maybe Saturday night. If I'm not too sore from mulching, and if *you're* not too sore from mulching."

"Lass, the day I'm too sore is the day they bury me." He kissed her hard and fast, and a thrill went through her body, heating her veins—a tease before the weekend, turning her week into a slow burn. Pulling away, there was a definite twinkle in his blue eyes. "Besides, if I'm too sore, I'll put you on top and make you do all the work."

"What if I'm too sore?"

Gavin shrugged nonchalantly.

"Then I'll spank you till you decide it's worth it."

Cracking up, Leah slapped her hand against his chest, still laughing when he caught her lips for another kiss. She felt like a teenager, making out in the parking lot with her boyfriend. It was fun, exciting, and way better than being a teenager. When she was a teen, orgasms had usually been self-applied, but she knew Gavin would be able to deliver.

Leaving her breathless, Gavin finally pulled away again, turning her around and giving her a swat on the butt.

"Text me when you get home, love."

"Alright." Leah got into her car, surprised at how sad she felt to be driving away from him. She blew him a kiss through the front window, laughing again when he pretended to catch it and put it in his pocket. The big doofus. Sometimes, he could be so silly, and it always caught her off guard... in a good way.

CHAPTER TWENTY-ONE

GAVIN

As staredowns went, Gavin didn't think he'd ever been in one where he worried he might be in danger of losing. Then again, he'd never had a staredown with a cat before. He hadn't spent all that much time around cats, and the cats he had known had mostly ignored him and everyone else.

Not Leah's cat.

Nope. The little orange devil jumped up onto the kitchen table while Gavin was waiting for Leah to finish changing into her 'gardening clothes' and sat his fuzzy little butt down right in front of Gavin and stared. Gavin stared back. Now, here they were. Silent. Unmoving. Unyielding.

"What are you doing?"

Gavin jumped. He'd been so focused staring down a cat, he hadn't heard Leah returning to the kitchen. Dammit. He'd also lost the stare down. The kitten gave him a smug look, then lifted its legs to start licking his arsehole. Lovely.

"Oliver and I were getting acquainted," Gavin said, getting to his feet. Leah looked at him suspiciously. Her hair was pulled back into a heavy braid and tucked under a bandana, and she was wearing overalls and a worn-out t-shirt. He'd dressed similarly, in an old pair of paint-stained jeans he didn't care about and a shirt that had seen better days. The overalls were a cute touch; he hadn't seen those before. Reaching out, he tugged on one of the straps. "Cute."

"Uh-uh," Leah scolded, twisting away from his fingers, still smiling. "Mulch first. Then you can play with the overalls. Maybe. Depending on how sweaty and dirty we get."

Gavin chuckled. As if a little sweat or dirt would stop him from getting what he wanted. He really did like the look of those baggy overalls. If he undid the two buttons holding the straps to the bib, they'd drop straight down, leaving her pants-less.

Why did people try to say overalls weren't sexy? Easy access like that was not a gift to be squandered.

"Let's go. There's a lot to be done," Leah said, herding him out the front door. Oliver followed them until she shooed him back. Gavin gave the cat a superior smirk before the door closed in the cat's face.

I may have lost the staredown, but I get to go outside with Leah.

Wait... was he seriously competing with a cat?

Don't answer that question.

"Okay, so I thought we'd start over there by the rhododendrons since they need the most mulch, then move our way around the rest of the garden," Leah said, pointing.

"Sounds good." It wasn't a lie exactly. There was something nice about hard work, even if it wasn't his preferred hard work. He could still take satisfaction in a job well done, and it made Leah happy, that was his true reward.

LEAH

Truth be told, Leah had expected a lot of sighs and complaints from Gavin throughout the process, but he almost seemed to be enjoying himself. Even better, they were making their way through the garden more than twice as fast as she would have on her own. With Gavin docilely following her instructions, she couldn't help but smile at the picture they posed. This was what she wanted—easy weekends doing regular household things and having a good time being together.

This was what she'd been missing all the years they were apart.

"We're doing great," she said as they came to the last flowerbed, Gavin toting the last bag of mulch. They were both sweaty, and they smelled, but she was looking forward to inviting him to shower off with her. It made her a little nervous, both the idea of putting forward the invitation and of having him in *this* house, which had been her sanctuary for so long, but if she wanted things to move forward, she needed to make herself vulnerable, too. "This would have taken me two days alone, but I'll be able to rest tomorrow."

Dropping the bag of mulch next to the flowerbed, Gavin rotated his shoulders and his neck, letting out a guttural groan. That was more like the noises she'd expected to hear from him all day, and she giggled, not feeling at all worried the noise was directed *at* her as she would have once done. She believed Gavin when he said he wanted to be here, even if the task might not be his favorite.

"I might have to cancel on Aiden," he said, shaking out the muscles he'd just stretched. "This was even more of a workout than I remembered. It can be my exercise for the weekend."

"Well, he'll still have Jax," Leah said, amused as she knelt down to rip open the bag and started scooping out the mulch. She'd never been much of a gym person; she'd much rather be doing something productive that also happened to give her a workout. Gardening was good exercise *and* made for a pretty final product. Then again, if her body built muscle and lost fat the way Gavin's did, she might be more inclined, but her extra pounds were a lot more stubborn than his. It was so unfair how easy it was for men to lose weight or bulk up when they wanted to!

Gavin snorted, picking up his shovel. "Jax barely comes to the gym anymore. Aiden will have to go on his own, or maybe he'll take the weekend off, too."

Blinking, Leah stilled.

"Jax hasn't been going to the gym?" Then why had he told Esther he was? That's what Esther had told her and Cyana. She wasn't misremembering that; she was sure of it. She wouldn't forget the reason her friend had been upset, even though Esther had said it was fine at the same time she'd been complaining.

"Haven't seen him in weeks. Why?" His tone was mild but curious, clearly not realizing something was amiss.

"Esther said he's been going every Sunday. She was venting about it, actually, since Jax hasn't had as much time for her lately, and going to the gym with you guys means he isn't around for hours on Sunday either." Worry started to rise as Leah spoke, and Gavin stared back at her with a puzzled expression. "Oh my God... has he been *lying* to her...?"

"Now, hold on, don't fly off the handle," Gavin said, which, of course, stirred her temper even more. She pressed her lips together, pushing away the emotion, telling herself he probably didn't realize how patronizing he sounded. "Maybe he's been going to a different gym on his own. We don't know what he's been doing, so we shouldn't jump to conclusions."

"I'm not jumping to conclusions," she countered hotly, stabbing her trowel into the mulch and spreading it around the flower in front of her. "He told her he's been at the gym with you and Aiden. Clearly, he hasn't been. So, regardless of what he's been doing, he's been lying to her."

The sigh that came from Gavin poked at her temper. She kept her head down, refusing to look up at him. His tone was already patronizing. If she looked up and he had condescension in his expression, she was going to go off on him, and she knew it.

She didn't understand how he could be so blasé about this.

"We don't know what he's doing," Gavin said firmly. Out of the corner of his eye, she could see him digging into the mulch, using the shovel to spread it around the opposite side of the flowerbed. "Maybe he had a good reason to tell Esther that."

"Yeah, well, I guess we'll find out soon."

The shovel stopped.

"What does that mean?" There was an odd note in Gavin's voice, one she didn't recognize, but alarm bells started going off.

"What do you mean, what does that mean?" Exasperated, Leah finally looked up at him, meeting his eyes. The expression on his face was inscrutable. "It means I'm going to ask him."

The exasperation she felt was mirrored in Gavin's eyes.

"It's not our business, Leah."

"Uh, if I find out my friend is being lied to, and she's hurting because of it, it becomes my business." She turned away from him, feeling her temper rising.

"He's not cheating on her."

Even the words made her blood freeze. She didn't want them to be true, not only because she couldn't see Jax as a cheater, but she didn't want that for Esther. If Jax *was* cheating, Leah and Cyana would work together to relieve him of his balls, but it would crush Esther. Deep down, that's what she was thinking. What other explanation did Gavin think there could be?

And how the hell did he think she was supposed to keep this knowledge from one of her best friends? It didn't matter that Jax was her friend, too. In this case, Esther was the injured party and deserved to know her husband was lying to her. That wasn't a secret Leah should have to keep. Expecting her to was unreasonable.

"We don't know that," she said tightly. "Which is why we should ask him. *I'll* ask him if you have a problem with doing so."

Ask for things for herself? Nope. Too scary. Ask a scary question to protect her friend? Yup. She was all over that.

Gavin made another frustrated noise. The mulch was really flying now from both of them as they worked out their emotions. This flowerbed was getting done much faster than the others, albeit in a somewhat messier fashion.

"I ask about things that are important." He gritted out the words between his teeth.

That did it. Leah stopped shoveling mulch. It was mostly done anyway.

"Jax lying to Esther isn't important?" She glared up at him. Seriously?

"We don't know what he said or why he said it. It's *not* our relationship. There is nothing good that can come from getting involved."

Getting to her feet, Leah gripped the trowel tightly as if holding on to it would help her keep a grip on her growing anger. Yeah, she knew their group of friends could sometimes split down the middle, the guys closer to each other than they were to the women and vice versa, but she hadn't thought he would be so callous.

"Well, then, you don't have to get involved," she snapped, knocking the mulch and dirt from her overalls. Now that she was already irritated, the grit and grime seemed more annoying than when she'd been enjoying herself.

"Do not ask Jax," Gavin ordered... and it definitely was an order. "Whatever's going on, it's clearly something he doesn't want people to know about."

"Oh, well, I'm so glad we had this *discussion*. Maybe if he didn't want people to know, he shouldn't have told such a stupid lie. It was bound to come out, eventually."

"Leah..." The warning in Gavin's voice made her want to snap. As if he had the right to make unilateral decisions for both of them. That was so like him. Dammit. Why had she thought this could still work out between them? When it came down to it, a tiger didn't change its stripes.

Gavin might be willing to work in the garden with her, but he was still trying to dictate to her. He still wasn't listening to her. He wasn't concerned about how Esther would feel about the situation, just like he hadn't thought about how Leah would feel.

She hadn't been unclear about what she wanted here, but he'd dismissed her out of hand as if her opinion didn't matter, like he had final say.

Yeah. She was done here.

His assistance had made a big difference, but this conversation had shown her things hadn't really changed. *He* hadn't really changed. Looking at the garden was going to be bittersweet this year—the memory of what could have been and how it had all fallen apart... again.

Better she knew now than later when she was even deeper into things and her hopes even further up.

"Thanks for coming over to help," she said, biting off the words and crossing her arms over her chest in an unwelcoming posture. Maybe she was being a 'guesser' by not asking him to leave, but clearly, he didn't care when she asked, anyway. "I appreciate it."

"Leah—"

"You'd better hurry home, so you can get to the club on time." It wasn't the first time she'd gotten rid of him by pointing that out, effectively ending a fight, and the reminder made a lump rise in her chest. Yeah, this felt an awful lot like how some of their old fights had ended... not in a good way.

Glancing down at his watch, Gavin cursed.

"We're not done talking about this," he said, surprising her by taking two steps forward to plant a kiss on her before she realized what was happening. "I'll see you later. Come to the club."

Yeah, no. The last thing she felt like doing tonight was having sex, but there he was, barking more orders and telling her what to do, not bothering to wait for an answer before getting in his car and driving away.

Pure tiredness seeped through her as she watched him go.

Do not go asking Jax.

Fine. It wasn't Jax she was concerned about, anyway. Turning to head into the house, she rubbed her forehead. She would take the time in the shower to think, but as soon as she was clean, she had a very uncomfortable phone call to make.

GAVIN

Watching the door and the clock, Gavin sighed when he realized Leah wasn't coming. It was too late in the evening.

Should he call her?

She was probably still pissed.

Why she was so upset, he wasn't sure. Did she really think Jax would cheat on Esther?

There was no way. There would be another explanation. Gavin was sure of it. Hell, if Jax was cheating on Esther, he'd eat his kilt.

At first, he hadn't realized that's where Leah's mind had gone because it was so unthinkable. Once he'd gotten it, he'd rejected the idea utterly. Jax was crazy about Esther. Not only that, he wasn't a cheater.

There had to be another explanation. If it really meant a lot to Leah, he supposed he could ask, but he didn't think Jax would take it well if Leah barged in with her accusation. Who would? It would be better if he asked Jax. Maybe he could do that tomorrow, then he could tell Leah how it went.

No, wait, he needed to include her.

He'd text her and let her know he was going to talk to Jax tomorrow, then hopefully, she wouldn't do anything rash.

Walking through the club, barely seeing any of the scenes happening around him, nodding to the members as if nothing was wrong, Gavin made his way back to his office. Sitting down in the chair, he picked up the cell phone from where he'd left it on his desk. No missed calls or texts from Leah, explaining she wasn't coming tonight.

She really was ticked.

While it went against the grain to insert himself into someone else's relationship without being explicitly asked for his opinion, Leah clearly felt Jax might actually be doing something wrong. Until she knew otherwise, she'd probably lump Gavin in with whatever she assumed Jax was doing, giving him the same amount of blame.

Which he could understand if he thought Jax was actually doing something wrong, but he didn't believe it. He also didn't understand how Leah could have so little faith in their friend. Was he in denial? No. Jax wouldn't. He knew Aiden and Gavin would kill him—and that was only if they got to him before Cyana. There was no way. Right?

Still, he probably should let Jax know he and Leah had figured out something was up. If only so Jax could explain himself to Esther because he deserved to be the one to do so, and Esther deserved to have him be the one to tell her what was going on. Whatever it was. Which definitely wasn't cheating.

Because Gavin would kill him.

Shaking his head, he tapped out a text message to Leah.

I'll talk to Jax tomorrow.

He almost added a line that he was sure there would be a reasonable explanation, but he deleted it before sending. Adding it wouldn't be helpful since he couldn't imagine it sounding anything other than snide, even if he meant it to be reassuring. A moment later, his phone buzzed.

Don't bother. I already told Esther.

"What the bloody hell?!"

CHAPTER TWENTY-TWO

Leah

When her phone went off again, Leah turned it to silent and tucked it under the pillow on her sofa, so they wouldn't be able to hear the vibrations. She wasn't taking texts *or* calls from Gavin right now. She was sure it wouldn't go over well. She was still too pissed, and she had probably royally ticked him off as well.

Oh, well. Shouldn't have tried to boss me around when it comes to my friends. Chicks before dicks! Hoes before bros! Clits before twits!

Yeah, she might be a little drunk, but the sentiment was on point.

"Gavin again?" Esther asked, her voice hollow. Oliver was on her lap, purring like a miniature motorboat while she stroked him, seeming to realize she needed comforting.

"Yup. Pretty sure he's ticked at me for telling you when he told me it wasn't our business."

"I'm glad you did." Esther didn't sound glad, and it hurt Leah's heart to see her like this. She knew she'd done the right thing, but she hated being the messenger of bad news. "I thought I was going crazy, that I was irrational or overly suspicious about all his extra hours at work, and now I feel... I don't know, vindicated? Like, if he's lying about the gym on Sundays, he's probably lying about his late evenings, too, right?"

"Maybe... I don't know." Leah scooted closer, slinging her arm around her friend. "Are you sure you don't want me to call Cyana? She could probably look into this for you."

"Not yet." Esther dropped her head, staring where she was petting Oliver rather than meeting Leah's eyes. "I love Cyana, but... she's going to go on the warpath, and I can't handle that right now. Maybe tomorrow." Leah had invited Esther to sleep over, putting particular emphasis on the 'sleeping over' part, and Esther had come immediately, likely thinking Leah had needed someone to vent to about Gavin. Well, that wasn't wrong, but it definitely hadn't been the focus.

Personally, Leah thought Cyana would be a little calmer and cooler rather than warpath-y, but it was true she was likely to be more action-oriented, and right now, Esther seemed to want to think. As hurt and angry as Leah was at Gavin, she knew it was so much worse for Esther right now.

Stupid Jax.

Leah wished she had him there in front of her so she could vent her anger on him. Even if he wasn't cheating, whatever his reason for lying, it wasn't worth making Esther feel like she was paranoid or finding out she wasn't. Both were hurtful.

Gavin didn't want them to get involved. Right, because Leah was supposed to walk around *knowing* Jax was lying, that Esther was already unhappy with how things were in their relationship, and pretend as if nothing was wrong. Maybe Gavin could do that. Hell, being oblivious to anything being wrong had basically been his M.O. during their relationship—but Leah couldn't.

Was he cheating? It was hard to imagine, but she couldn't think of any other reason for how long he'd been sneaking around and lying to Esther. She might have trouble picturing him cheating on Esther, but even if he wasn't, he'd still been lying to her. Neglecting her. Pretending he was somewhere, he wasn't. Hurting her by his absence.

Unacceptable.

If their anniversary was coming up or something, Leah might have worried she'd jumped the gun and he was planning something for Esther, but that had been several months ago. What else could he be doing?

"I don't know what to do," Esther admitted. "Is it wrong that part of me wants to go home and pretend like nothing is happening?"

"I don't think that's wrong at all." Leah gave Esther's shoulders a squeeze, her own heart aching in sympathy. "And if that's the choice you make, I will accept that. I just wanted you to have that choice."

Granted, she would think Esther was making the wrong choice, but it was Esther's to make. She didn't think her friend would be able to live like that for very long, especially if Jax kept up his late nights and going who-knows-where on Sundays.

"I'm glad I do... I just wish I knew what to do." Esther rubbed her forehead, and Leah pulled her into her arms as she started to cry. Tears sparked in Leah's eyes. She didn't have any easy answers for her friend. The only one who truly had answers was Jax, but at least now Esther knew she wasn't imagining things.

GAVIN

It was a restless night after he got home. He'd wanted to leave the club and going to Leah's, but he'd ultimately decided against it. She wasn't picking up her phone, so he didn't think showing up at her house would make things better, especially when they were both still angry.

Dammit. He'd thought they'd agreed to talk more about what to do before taking any action. Leah certainly hadn't said differently when he'd said they'd talk later, but then she'd gone behind his back and contacted Esther.

Spending most of the night tossing and turning hadn't helped matters.

There was a sick feeling in the pit of his gut that had nothing to do with their friends and everything to do with him and Leah. Not only were they not on the same page, but he didn't even know what she was thinking and had a feeling that was a bad thing.

Why hadn't she waited until they'd had more time to talk things through?

He sort of understood. She was protective of her friends, and it wasn't like he *wasn't*, but he was willing to extend more grace to Jax than she was apparently, which surprised him.

Maybe that was his real issue. Not only that the situation was now entirely out of control, with no hope of figuring out what was going on before someone got hurt, but he didn't understand where Leah was coming from. He wanted to, but it didn't make sense.

Before he tried calling her again, he made himself drink two cups of coffee, eat breakfast, and take a shower, all of which had the salutary effect of waking him up and improving his mood. At the very least, he felt refreshed and alert. To his surprise and relief, she picked up the phone, although her tone was fairly hostile.

"Hello."

"Leah." Her name came out as a sigh, tinged with resignation but also relief. Gavin really hadn't been sure she'd pick up. Some of his temper faded hearing her voice. "How is Esther?"

"She's okay." Her tone was softer, less defensive, a little sad. "She slept over last night, and she left to go home about ten minutes ago. That's why I answered the phone—I was going to call you, anyway. She's asked us not to say anything to Jax while she figures out how to confront him... or if she even wants to."

Gavin rubbed at a spot in the middle of his forehead, which suddenly felt sore, like a precursor to a headache.

"Ah, so what I wanted to do, but for both of them?" Crap, he knew that wasn't helpful the moment he said it, but seriously? They could have done that last night, then they'd be keeping things from *both* of their friends instead of just one of them. Now, when Jax found out, he'd feel like they were taking Esther's side since he hadn't been given a heads up.

He could picture Leah sitting with her arms crossed defensively, anticipating his reaction. Unfortunately, knowing she was expecting him to be angry didn't do anything to cool him down. It felt as if she was goading him.

"Maybe you could spend the rest of our lives pretending like you didn't know Jax was lying to Esther, but I couldn't," Leah snapped, and even over the phone, he could feel her bristling.

He let his head hang back, then rolled it forward, trying to loosen the suddenly tight muscles. While he didn't do the whole 'count to ten' thing, he did take a moment before responding, gathering himself and trying to keep his cool.

"That's not what I asked you to do. I asked you to *wait*, so we could talk about it later and come to a decision *together*."

"You didn't *ask* anything. You ordered me not to say anything to Jax. You ordered me to wait and talk to you later. You don't get to order me around when it comes to my friends, and you don't get to make unilateral decisions for both of us."

"Oh, but you do? Maybe I ordered you to wait and talk to me later, but you didn't, did you? Instead, *you* made the unilateral decision to talk to Esther. *You* made the irrevocable, unilateral decision, and you didn't even have the courtesy to tell me you were going to. You couldn't wait *one* day, so we could talk more about what to do?"

The sudden silence on her end meant she was in a raging temper or his words had hit home. Since they were on the phone, he couldn't tell which. He rubbed his forehead again. He should have had more coffee.

LEAH

As angry as she was, a spurt of guilt popped up, realizing Gavin was right. No, she hadn't liked the way he'd *told* her not to confront Jax nor liked the way he'd *told* her they'd talk later, but he wasn't entirely wrong either. Even though she hadn't liked the *way* he'd told her, she could have sucked that up and waited until they had more time to talk. Until they'd both had more time to think. She'd been running high on indignation and anger at both him and Jax.

175

Yes, she'd told Esther because she thought Esther deserved to know, but she couldn't deny there had been a bit of self-righteousness as well. How *dare* Gavin order her around when it came to her friendships?

She wasn't entirely wrong either.

"Esther deserved to know."

"I don't disagree, but I also think we could have waited. Last night, I came to the decision I would talk to Jax because it seemed important to you. I *don't* believe he's cheating on Esther, but I would have told him his lie was out, and whatever he's doing, he needs to come clean with her, or we would talk to her."

Chewing her lower lip, Leah leaned back against the couch where she was sitting. Oliver was on her lap, tiny claws incessantly kneading her thigh while she stroked his soft fur. He'd been pretty attached to Esther until she left as if he'd sensed she needed his comfort, but when Leah had answered the phone, he'd jumped up onto her lap.

She didn't want to admit it, but what Gavin was saying made sense. Some of what he said still irked her.

"So, you eventually came to the same decision I had. But *I* wasn't allowed to do anything until you agreed with me."

The frustrated noise Gavin made wasn't quite a growl.

"It would have been nice if you'd waited as I wanted you to. I'm sorry about the way I phrased it, that it came out as an order. I wanted time to think. I didn't think that was unreasonable."

"It wasn't." Oliver purred, and she took some comfort in that. "But ordering me around was. It made me feel as if you were making decisions for both of us again, and I didn't get an equal say—or any say at all. I can't live like that again."

"I wish you had said something. You let me go off, thinking we were going to talk about it later, and instead, you went behind my back and told Esther." His voice was quiet but firm, and Leah squirmed uncomfortably, knowing he was right. She was, too, but she *could* have waited to talk to him until deciding whether to talk to Esther or Jax. "I didn't get any say in that."

It might have been better to do things Gavin's way, something she hadn't even considered. Yeah, his approach to Jax sounded far more sympathetic than hers would be, but on the other hand, that might not be a bad thing. She wanted to smack Jax upside the head for hurting Esther, but that wouldn't actually solve anything, even though it would feel good.

This was annoying. They were both right and both wrong. Leah wasn't sure how she felt about that. It was hard to keep up righteous self-indignation in the face of the points Gavin was making.

"I don't want to make you feel as if you can't have a say, and I didn't mean to order you around. I was upset and pressed for time. That's not an excuse. I know I reverted back to some of my old habits, but you did as well. Rather than talking to me or even waiting to talk to me, you made a decision and went and did it. I can't help but as though you've been waiting for me to fail, waiting for an excuse to shove me back out of your life."

Ouch. Her chest physically ached with the accuracy of that shot. Yeah, she'd been upset and angry at him last night, but there had also been a bit of underlying relief—*the other shoe had finally dropped.*

"So, what do we do now?" she asked tiredly. "Do we just keep going around in circles? Because that's what it feels like." Last night, if they'd talked, she knew this would have been a much hotter argument, but her temper had some time to cool. Comforting Esther and wondering if she'd done the right thing by telling her, especially when Esther had decided to wait before deciding what *she* was going to do, had done even more to diminish her irritation. "When it comes to this relationship, it doesn't feel like the odds are *ever* in our favor."

"Never tell me the odds."

Leah laughed, a short, sharp sound. Trust Gavin to meet her *Hunger Games* reference with Han Solo. It was one of the things she liked about him. She didn't know if they could make this work, no matter how they felt about each other. Didn't last night prove it?

Now she could see, *neither* of them had really changed. Even knowing their old habits and how badly they'd affected each other, their first argument, they'd slipped right back into them.

"I'd like to make an appointment with Dr. Silverwood for us

tomorrow if that works for you. Otherwise, we can go as usual on Wednesday. If you want to."

"What if I don't want to?" she asked, more out of curiosity and to buy herself some time to think. That was not the answer she'd been expecting. She didn't know *what* she'd been expecting, to be honest, but Gavin's suggestion they make an appointment to see their couples' counselor right away had not been it.

"Then I'll go on my own. Whether or not we work out, I think she's been good for me. But I hope you'll come with me. I'm not ready to give up on us. If you are... well, I won't blame you. I know you were reluctant to start with, and I'm grateful you gave me another chance."

He sounded so tired. Resigned. Unhappy. Not as if he'd given up, exactly, only that he realized he *couldn't* control her decision. He was leaving it entirely up to her.

For some reason, that made her want to run, but Leah squashed the emotion.

Yeah, last night, he'd reverted to some of his bossiest inclinations, and she'd felt dismissed, but he hadn't been the only one to backslide. Yet, he still wanted to try. He wasn't giving up.

Oliver butted his head against the bottom of her chin as if encouraging her to make the decision she knew, deep down in her heart of hearts, she really wanted.

"Yeah. Let's see if we can see Dr. Silverwood tomorrow."

The only way things *would* really be different would be if she and Gavin worked together. He was trying. He'd apologized, explained himself, and wanted to go to therapy, leaving her with very little to be angry about, really. Going to see Dr. Silverwood rather than cutting and running was definitely different for her.

CHAPTER TWENTY-THREE

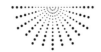

GAVIN

Mondays at the Outlands on the restaurant level were pretty slow, which was welcome after the weekend, but today, Gavin wished it was a little busier to help keep his mind off things.

He kept replaying his and Leah's argument in his head and wanting to kick himself. While he was the boss in the bedroom, and even occasionally sometimes out of it, he honestly hadn't meant to order her around. He'd been reacting rather than acting. That didn't mean it was okay, but he was hoping she understood enough to be forgiving.

Forgiving her for going to Esther was a little easier after they'd talked. She wanted to protect her friend and had probably been reacting to Gavin's dictates. It hadn't even occurred to him until later, she *had* actually followed his order not to confront Jax. She'd gone straight to Esther, who he'd said nothing about. He still wasn't sure if she'd realized that.

If she hadn't, he wasn't going to bring it up.

The hours slowly ticked by until he was finally able to hurry off to Dr. Silverwood's office. If his employees were surprised by how fast he dashed out the door, no one said anything to him.

By some chance of fate, Leah pulled into the parking lot right after him. He could see her in his rearview mirror and caught the moment she realized she was directly behind him. It was hard to tell how she felt about it.

Getting out of the car, he walked to the sidewalk, waiting for her to join him. He supposed he could have gone in on his own while she sat in the car fiddling with her purse as if to give him time to do so, but that didn't sit right with him. So, he waited. After a few minutes, she got out of the car, her lips pursed as if she was annoyed with him for waiting.

For some reason, that made him grin. The corner of her mouth tipped up before she pushed it down again.

He knew she hadn't really expected him to go inside without her, and *she* knew that, too. The fiddling with her purse had been to give her time, but she wasn't actually annoyed with him for waiting.

Dressed in a blue pantsuit, her thick blonde hair pulled into a braid that trailed over her shoulder, she looked like business-Elsa from that kids' movie. Gavin kinda liked it. Then again, he'd always liked her dressed up in her suits. She looked so prim and proper, it made him want to peel them off to find the wild woman underneath.

By contrast, he was wearing his usual jeans and an Outlands bar shirt. Today, more than ever, it emphasized both the differences between them and how things hadn't really changed over the years on the surface. Ten years ago, if they'd gone to counseling, they would have shown up wearing very similar outfits to what they wore now.

The difference was, Gavin was older, less prideful, and far more determined to make things work out this time—because he knew exactly what he had to lose.

"Hello, love." He held out his hand, offering it to her, wondering if she would take it.

She only hesitated a moment before her fingers settled into his, though she didn't come in for a kiss. At least, she was holding his hand. That was a small step forward.

"Hi," Leah said almost shyly, averting her eyes and not meeting his gaze. He gave her fingers a squeeze and saw her relax as he led her inside.

LEAH

Sitting next to Gavin on the couch, Leah was very aware of his proximity, part of the reason she'd kept a little space between them before. It was so easy to feel overshadowed by his presence. On the other hand, she also found the strength emanating from him to be comforting, and she needed that today.

Besides, she didn't think he was going to relinquish her hand once she'd give him hold of it. Deep down, she didn't want him to.

With as many years as she'd spent hung up on this man, she *wanted* them to work, but she was also afraid of wasting more time if they ultimately didn't. It felt as if nothing had changed, that they were going around the same issues over and over again, which was what she'd been afraid of.

"It sounds as if you two inadvertently hit on a hot topic. Because of your past relationship, there are going to be things that seem small but that can blow up into something much bigger. It's actually triggering past emotions, and those can get all tangled up in your present emotions." Dr. Silverwood sounded almost as if she was giving a school lecture on the topic, but it still struck home with Leah. Glancing at Gavin, who was doing the same back to her, she realized it did for him as well.

They'd both poked at old wounds and reverted to old behaviors. Not exactly encouraging.

Apparently, Dr. Silverwood disagreed.

"What's good is you both recognized what had happened, even though it was after the fact, and you were able to talk through it together." Dr. Silverwood beamed at them approvingly.

Oh… Leah hadn't thought about it like that.

In the past, she and Gavin had never had a phone conversation like they had yesterday morning. They'd argued, yelled, then gone back through it again until she'd shut down because she couldn't take it anymore. Then had come the silent treatment.

Yesterday's conversation on the phone had felt incredibly circular because while they were talking about how they'd reverted back to old habits, the conversation itself was something entirely new. They'd talked through it, both of them acknowledging the other's points and being able to see the other's perspective. She'd understood where Gavin was coming from and felt like he'd understood her.

They might not have entirely agreed with what the other person wanted to do, but that wasn't insurmountable. If they hadn't blown up at each other the evening before—if she had waited to talk to him rather than reacting—they might have even worked through it together. The tightness in her chest loosened, and she even felt a little warmer inside.

Gavin squeezed her fingers again, and she squeezed his back without thinking. This felt... better. Like they were working together as a team. Which was something she hadn't felt in far longer than they'd been divorced. Her heart felt lighter after hearing Dr. Silverwood point out what they'd done *right* and knowing she didn't think they were a lost cause.

"Where do we go from here?" Gavin asked, echoing the question Leah had asked him last night. He hadn't loosened his grip on her hand, as if he was afraid she was going to sneak away if he let go.

She leaned a little closer, and their upper arms touched. Saw him glance at her out of the corner of her eye but didn't look back at him, still watching Dr. Silverwood, waiting for her response.

"Forward. If you want to. I think you two have a good start, but there will be times when old habits happen. What's important is you recognize and work past them. I'm sure it felt like a regression, but from everything you've told me, I see this as progress. We'll keep working on the communication. I think it's great how fully committed you two are to making this work."

Fully committed... right.

Except Leah hadn't been, had she?

GAVIN

They left Dr. Silverwood's office the way they'd come in, hand-in-hand. Gavin felt much lighter and more hopeful than he had the past twenty-four hours. He really hadn't known what to expect from talking to Dr. Silverwood today, but her assessment had far exceeded his wildest hopes.

In some ways, suggesting they come to talk to her had been *his* last-ditch effort to make things work, the same way it had been for Leah all those years ago. Yes, he wished he'd done it then, but he was glad they were doing it now and doubly glad Leah hadn't turned him down when he'd made the suggestion.

Something was bugging Leah. He could tell. The closer they got to their cars, the more jittery she seemed. Maybe worried about how to say goodbye? They'd agreed they wanted to keep working on things with Dr. Silverwood, which meant they were going to keep seeing each other, but things still felt awkward.

Well, he'd be able to soothe her on that front. Gavin planned to get a kiss before she left to make up for the way their time together on Saturday ended.

Walking her to her car door, Gavin pulled her around to face him, wrapping his arms around her waist. Leah immediately tipped her head back, eyes already closing as he leaned in for the kiss. She sighed against his lips, melting into him with little resistance, and some of Gavin's nerves relaxed. He kept the kiss gentle, seductive rather than demanding, and Leah responded in kind. When they finally broke apart, he smiled down at her, but she still looked nervous.

"Um, would you like to get together tonight?" she blurted before he could say anything, and Gavin's smile widened. If that was what she was nervous about, he was happy to assuage her worry. Especially since it was a Monday night, and the Outlands didn't need him on the floor. He'd hand everything over to Trey, the night manager.

"Sure." His fingers stroked over her back. "I'll take you out?"

If anything, her nerves seemed to increase, and she took a deep breath. Gavin tilted his head as he looked down at her, studying her and trying to figure out what was causing her consternation.

"I meant... would you like to come over to my place... tonight? For dinner and um, a sleepover."

"I would love to." He frowned. She seemed more amped up than a simple invitation would explain. He was amused by her calling it a sleepover. "Are you sure? I don't want to come over if you're not comfortable having me there." She'd once told him the reason she'd moved out of their house had been because she hadn't been able to get away from the memories.

"I am. Sorta. It's kind of a big step." She smiled up at him a little shakily, but there was determination in her blue eyes. "I was going to invite you to come shower with me on Saturday before we got off track. What Dr. Silverwood said about commitment and what you said about me waiting for something to go wrong, both of those things are true. I haven't been fully committed because I've been waiting for something to go wrong, but we can't go forward if I'm holding back. And I want to go forward."

"Lass, ye have no idea how relieved I am to hear ye say that." Gavin chuckled, curving his fingers around her jaw and brushing another kiss over her lips. Leah relaxed further and giggled. "I would love to come over this evening... and have a *sleepover*. Shall I bring the nail polish? Can we have a pillow fight? Oof." He grunted when she elbowed him in the gut.

"Your sense of humor gets weird at the oddest times," she said, shaking her head, but her eyes sparkled with mirth. This felt like the good times, with flirtatious banter back and forth.

"You bring it out in me." He dropped another kiss to her lips before letting her go. "I'll see you tonight, love."

"See you tonight." She looked reluctant to let him go, which Gavin took as a good sign.

Opening the car door for her, he waited until she got inside, and a thought occurred to him, and he paused.

"Leah? Should I bring my toy bag?"

Pink filled her cheeks in a hot blush, which he loved to see, and she nodded.

"Yes, please."

CHAPTER TWENTY-FOUR

LEAH

Before Gavin arrived at her house, Leah texted Esther. She'd been trying to give her friend space but was getting worried she hadn't heard from her.

Hey, hun, I wanted to check in and see how you're doing today.

Thankfully, it didn't take long for Esther to text back, or else Leah probably would have spent all night fretting. She was already worried she hadn't done the right thing, especially after hearing Gavin's plan. It would have probably been better for Jax to talk directly to Esther.

She had the feeling she was angrier at Jax than Gavin was, which irked her a little, but she understood it didn't mean Gavin didn't care about Esther, but he assumed Jax had some kind of good reason for lying. Leah wasn't so trusting.

I'm fine. Everything is normal. I'm going to wait and see.

The desire for action—and answers—made Leah's skin itch, but it wasn't her life. She didn't have two kids in high school. Yeah, she'd ultimately divorced Gavin when Mitch was still in high school, but that had been a long time coming at that point. While Esther hadn't exactly been blindsided by finding out Jax had been lying to her, it wasn't as if they'd had ongoing issues for years.

I'm here for you, whatever you need.

Leah typed out the response, keeping it vague the same way Esther had, and sent it before heading to the kitchen to start dinner. Oliver wandered in, and she fed him before she started cooking, which made him happy. She'd decided to keep things simple tonight —tacos, rice, and salad. Taco night had always been one of both her and Gavin's favorites. Plus, it gave her plenty to do since she liked to make her guacamole fresh.

She knew some of her nervousness came from having Gavin come over, but it was the right step. If she kept putting it off, keeping him out of parts of her life, trying to protect herself, she wasn't really committing to giving him a second chance. Despite the setback, he really had been making a real effort.

She was also anxious because she wanted him to punish her. They'd both been right, but they'd also both been wrong, and Leah truly wished she'd waited to talk to Gavin before talking to Esther. She'd completely cut him out of the decision-making—what she'd felt he'd done to her—and the hypocrisy didn't sit well with her. Neither did feeling like a part of the reason she'd told Esther had been to prove something to Gavin. Yes, she'd truly felt Esther deserved to know, but she also knew her rush to tell her friend had been motivated by her reaction to how she'd felt Gavin was treating her.

That wasn't okay.

Thankfully, BDSM gave her both a way to purge her guilt and soothe her conscience. Eventually, she'd need to apologize to Esther for her less-than-generous motivations behind why she'd insisted Esther come over that night.

The doorbell rang while the meat was still sizzling, and she hurried to answer it.

"Hey! Come on in. Sorry... cooking." Giving a surprised Gavin a quick kiss before rushing back to the kitchen, she was far too aware of all the nervous butterflies fluttering through her stomach as if they were having a rave. Picking up the spoon, she gave the meat a quick stir.

"Smells great," Gavin said as he followed her into the kitchen. "Mmmm, tacos."

Coming up behind her, he pressed a kiss to the back of her neck, making her shiver. Hand on her hip, he leaned over to see what she was doing, the heat of his body behind her sending all sorts of tingles up and down her nerve endings.

Yes, please.

Except he was making it hard to concentrate. Giggling, Leah bumped him with her hip.

"Be useful and make the salad." She tilted her head toward the pile of vegetables on the counter.

"Yes, ma'am." Chuckling, Gavin gave her hip one last caress before moving to do her bidding. A little smile curved Leah's lips as she watched him out of the corner of her eye. While she'd changed from her work clothes into something more comfortable, he was still in his, but she appreciated a man in well-fitted jeans and a t-shirt, especially when they looked like Gavin.

GAVIN

Dinner was comfortable. Some people might not think it was exciting, but to Gavin, it was as though he'd found his favorite old pair of jeans and discovered they still fit perfectly.

They veered away from heavier topics, like Esther and Jax or their past issues, and focused on the day-to-day issues—business at the Outlands, Leah's current project at work, and the other regular things that made up their days. It was wonderfully normal, making him realize how much he'd missed meals like this with her.

Not just because she was a damn good cook, either.

"You inhaled that. Did you even chew?" She raised her eyebrow, laughter dancing in her eyes.

"It was good." He shrugged, unapologetic. Leaning back, he patted his stomach. "I rarely cook for myself, mostly eat at the Outlands, so I don't get home cooking often."

"Well, that can't be healthy." A note of scolding entered her voice. "You'd better be eating some salads now and then."

"More of them the older I get." Chuckling, he studied her as she pushed the last bits of lettuce around her plate. "I can't eat the way I used to if I want to keep my girlish figure."

"Oh, please." Leah snorted laughter, shaking her head. "You look great, and you know it." She was clearly enjoying herself, but there was an odd edge to her demeanor.

"What's going through your mind, love?" He leaned over to put his hand on hers, stilling its nervous movement. "I don't have to stay over tonight. We can keep it to dinner for now."

"No, that's not..." Letting go of her fork, she took a deep breath and met his gaze. "I want you to punish me tonight."

Gavin blinked. That wasn't what he'd expected.

"Why?" He asked more of a way to buy time, so he could get his thoughts in order. Now that she'd said what she wanted, he had his suspicions why, but her desires didn't line up with what he'd been thinking for the evening. While he'd brought his toy bag and a change of clothes, he'd left both of them in his car, so she wouldn't feel pressured. If she didn't change her mind, he'd been anticipating a night of fun, sensuous play to reconnect, not a punishment scene.

"You were right. I should have waited to talk to you. I let emotion and our past overrule my common sense. I was also a hypocrite since I did what I was accusing you of. While I still think Esther had the right to know, she didn't have to be told immediately. I could have waited. Should have waited." Her voice was tight, unhappy. The atmosphere in the room had changed, becoming heavy with emotion.

Damn. She really did feel guilty. Gavin's brain was already shifting gears, restructuring the scene he'd planned in his head to fit what his submissive needed.

"You weren't the only one letting your emotions and past behavior rule you," he pointed out. "I gave you an order without even realizing it. I also didn't take the time to ask why you were so adamant about it or listened to you at the moment."

"Yes, and you feel bad, I can tell." Leah seemed calmer now that she'd stated what she needed. Her blue eyes were filled with certainty that he would give her what she craved. "I need more. Please, Master."

Bloody hell.

That was a punch right to the gut. Closing his eyes for a brief moment, he took the time to savor the sound of her calling him 'Master' again. It was more than unexpected—it was something he'd never really expected to hear again.

"Alright then, naughty girl. Let's get this kitchen cleaned up so I can deal with you."

LEAH

Completely naked and bent over the edge of her bed, waiting to be spanked, Leah probably shouldn't feel quite so Zen. She felt calm. Ready. Eager.

Strong fingers caressed her buttocks before giving her right cheek a little slap, hard enough to make her shiver. The sting of the pain zinged pleasantly through her.

"What are you sorry for, *mo chridhe?*"

The endearment made her heart sing, as much as calling him 'Master.' Yes, she knew 'happily-ever-after' wasn't as easy as deciding to commit to each other—if it was, they would already be living theirs after getting married—but she really thought they had a chance. Their second chance, which made it even more meaningful to her. After being hung up for ten years on the man she'd divorced, she knew how precious chances like this were. So many things had lined up exactly right in order for them to have this one.

As she started to speak, she felt the tip of a plug nudging against her anus, and it made her shiver.

"I'm sorry for not waiting to talk to you."

The plug pushed in, stretching the entrance, the tight ring of muscles burning in protest.

"I'm sorry for telling Esther without giving us a chance to talk more about what to do."

The toy delved deeper, stretching her wider, and Leah groaned. Her fingers flexed on the bed, toes trying to curl as the plug filled her, burning pleasantly with every centimeter. She panted for breath as it moved, trying to concentrate on what she was saying, despite the physical distraction.

"I'm sorry for reacting, rather than thinking through what I really wanted."

The plug settled firmly inside her, the widest part pushing past her entrance, and her muscles clenched around the little gap between the base and the bulb. Leah moaned, shuddering, cheek pressed against the soft comforter on her bed as her body finished adjusting to the intruder.

"Good girl," Gavin said, tugging gently on the base of the plug, so it pressed against her from the opposite direction. "Now I'm going to spank you, and when I'm done, I'm going to fuck this pretty little arse."

She whimpered. She loved it when he talked dirty, but there was something about anal sex that always made her feel particularly naughty, and he knew it. For them, funishment usually meant anal. It didn't matter how many times she'd had his cock in her ass, every time she still felt like a 'dirty girl.' Just the thought made her pussy throb in excitement, which was fairly ironic.

Smack!

The hard slap of his hand against her ass made her jerk forward, though there was nowhere to go because of the bed. It might be more on the 'funishment' than the 'punishment' end of the scale, but it still hurt. Her ass clenched around the plug, which suddenly felt twice as invasive because she knew what it would be eventually replaced with.

His hand came down hard on the opposite cheek, the crisp swats moving back and forth between them in a stinging chorus of pleasurable pain. Gasping, Leah's hips moved, pushing up to meet his hand, crying out when his palm landed on her ass. The skin of her bottom warmed, heating her blood and ramping up her libido with excitement.

The slaps moved up and down, making sure to cover every spot of her curvy mounds. When his fingers flicked against the base of the plug, the vibrations ricocheted through her. A hard slap on her pussy made her cry out, pushing her onto her toes as her tears began to soak the comforter beneath her, then she was needily, eagerly, arching her back, slightly begging for more.

CHAPTER TWENTY-FIVE

GAVIN

The soft, sweet cries coming from Leah's lips as he spanked her had Gavin's cock filling and thickening with anticipation. The creamy skin of her arse was slowly turning a beautiful bright pink under his hand, the surface warming with every slap he laid on it.

As spankings went, it wasn't particularly harsh—he didn't have it in him to truly punish her when they'd both been in the wrong—but it would be enough to help relieve the guilt she clearly felt. Especially once he got his cock in her arse. He'd learned long ago nothing else put Leah into quite so submissive a mindset.

There was an intimacy to the act that appealed greatly to both of them, as well as its taboo nature. She had a beautiful arse, so it was no surprise he loved fucking it. Saving it for 'naughty girl' sex made it even more special. He'd plugged her regularly, but that wasn't really the same.

Slapping his hand against her already pink cheek, he watched her flesh ripple from the impact, her buttocks bouncing and squeezing in reaction before relaxing again. Between the twin mounds, the black base of the plug looked almost ominous. He'd have to buy her some new, prettier ones. After their divorce, he'd switched to more utilitarian options, but he'd like to see sparkling jewels winking back at him again. He'd missed them.

His hand slapped her pussy, making her shriek, but his fingers came away damp.

"Such a naughty girl, aren't ye?" He chuckled, slapping her pussy again, making sure the tips of his fingers connected with her clit. Leah went up on her toes and fell back down, whimpering. "You're turned on because you want my cock in your arse."

Leah moaned again, turning her head, so her face was pressed fully against the mattress, hidden from him, but he knew she was blushing, which made him chuckle again. He loved that he could still make her blush at their age, after all the perverse and filthy things he'd done to her over the years.

Running his fingers up the slick seam of her pussy to the base of the plug, he twisted it, knowing it would add to the sensations already running riot through. She squirmed as he twirled the base, pumping it just enough for her to feel the movement without pulling it out of her. His cock throbbed in eagerness to replace the plug, remembering how tightly she'd grip him when he was buried deep within her.

"Tell me you want my cock in yer arse, naughty girl."

Another whimper. More squirming. But no words. Gavin kept playing with the plug with one hand, and his other hand came down on her arse with a loud crack. Shrieking, Leah wriggled.

"I... I want your cock in my arse.... I mean ass."

Gavin brought his hand down again, on the same spot he'd just spanked, making her buck and scream.

"Almost correct, love. You were missing something, though." He pumped the plug a little more firmly, letting it begin to stretch the muscles of her entrance before pushing it back in again. Leah moaned again, but they both knew what he was asking her for, and she obliged.

"I want your cock in my ass, Master."

Fuck, hearing her call him that... Warmth filled his chest, along with relief. He hadn't been sure whether she'd call him 'Sir' or 'Master,' since either would have been entirely acceptable. He'd hoped they wouldn't be going back to 'Sir' after she'd already used 'Master' earlier.

LEAH

"Good girl." Gavin's voice rasped, and she knew he was as affected by her use of his title as she was.

Especially when he was about to fuck her ass, which made her even more submissive, more vulnerable to him than ever. Part of her was still scared, still worried things wouldn't work out, but she didn't want it to become a self-fulfilling prophecy. If she held back, if she wasn't really giving them a true chance, of course, they would fail.

Calling him 'Master' again, having him in this house, was symbolic. Maybe no one else in the world would consider it a grand romantic gesture, but for her, that's what both of those things were. He was back in her space, and she was acknowledging who she wanted him to be in her life.

Her love. Her happy ending. Her Master.

The plug twisted inside her, lighting up all the sensitive nerve endings around her entrance as if he was setting off kinky fireworks inside her. Then he pulled, and this time, he didn't push the toy back in. Her opening stretched, the burn much slighter than when the plug had gone in, and she felt the odd, slick sensation of it being removed, leaving her so very empty.

Her pussy spasmed, knowing what was coming next.

"Reach back and hold yourself open for me, *mo chridhe.*"

Leah wanted to whimper again, but this was part of the 'punishment.' She didn't really think she had a humiliation kink, other than this one act. Something about parting her butt cheeks for him, knowing he didn't need her to but was ordering her to because it would expose her further and make her even more aware of what he was about to do, flat out did it for her.

The heat under her palms from her spanking, the way her fingers dug into her soft flesh, knowing how exposed she was to his eyes as he looked down at her from behind—everything about this supremely submissive position and the perverse nature of the act roused her. The tip of his cock pressed against her forbidden entrance, slick and hot and slightly painful as it began to push in.

Whimpering, she arched her back, her fingers digging further into her buttocks as Gavin's cock pushed deeper, stretching her open. The plug never truly prepared her for anal sex because the shape of the plug was so different from his cock. The plug was tapered and had a notch where the tight ring of her sphincter could close up fairly tight and rest.

Gavin's cock was thick from the tip to the base, keeping her stretched wide open without surcease as it slid through the ring. The blunt head of his cock delved far deeper inside her than the plug, filling her in a way the toy never did. The combination of pleasure and pain as he penetrated her was sinfully erotic.

With her hands splayed over her buttocks, there was no need for him to touch her anywhere else, so the only thing connecting them was his cock slowly invading her clenching hole. There was nothing else for her to focus on, no other thing happening to her body for her to distract her. It was disturbingly intimate. Wickedly arousing.

His hands finally curved around her hips as his body pressed against her hot cheeks, his cock fully buried inside her. Leah squirmed, uncomfortably full and perversely aroused. Between her thighs, her clit throbbed with the need to be touched.

"You may release."

Her hands let go of her buttocks, almost missing the heat as soon as her palms began to cool. She moaned as he drew back, the sensation always uncomfortable and odd, followed immediately by him plunging back in, filling her all over again with a slightly painful thrust.

She could feel every inch of his slick cock as he began his slow, steady thrusts, his hands pressing her down, pinning her to the bed so he could fuck her ass. Squirming beneath him, her clit pulsed, pussy clenching emptily while he rode her from behind. With every deep stroke, her arousal climbed higher and higher, even though he wasn't touching her pussy.

Something about being used for his pleasure turned her on so much, it didn't matter he wasn't touching her clit or pussy, her body responded as if he was. There was a spot deep inside her, his cock rubbed every time he impaled her, like a g-spot that wound her arousal into a tighter and tighter coil within her core.

The orgasm rolled through her like a tidal wave, pulling back, then crashing over her, carrying her along its crest and leaving her grabbing the sheets, trying to find purchase while the sensations dragged her along.

GAVIN

Leah's cries changed, her muscles clenching around his cock, and Gavin knew she'd managed to orgasm without stimulation to her pussy. His own arousal surging, he slid his hand down between her body and the bed, his fingers finding her clit and strumming the tiny bud as he rode her arse harder and faster.

She bucked beneath him, choking on the sounds of her ecstasy as he added to the pleasure driving her climax. The tight grasp of her muscles increased, spasming around his cock, squeezing and clenching, bringing him to his own peak.

With a loud groan, he buried himself, his cock pulsing with every spurt of pleasure, flooding her bowels with hot fluid until they were both completely spent.

Panting for breath, he let himself enjoy lying on her back for a moment, enough of his weight on his arms to keep from crushing her. The heat from her bottom warmed his groin, her muscles still spasming as his cock slowly shrank inside her. He felt, more than heard, her small whimper and pushed himself up, rolling onto the bed and reaching out to pull her with him.

Slightly sweaty and completely satiated, he cuddled her close, feeling more at peace than ever. Their breathing and heart rates slowed together, her hand stroking through his chest hair in silence, his fingers tracing tiny patterns on her shoulder.

He felt her head move against his arm. Twisting his own to meet her gaze, a small smile curving his lips. Leah smiled back, almost shyly, looking so very much like the young woman he'd met and fallen in love with, it was as if the years had fallen away, and they were back at the beginning.

Weren't they, in a way? A new beginning to the next chapter of their lives. Hopefully, a better chapter than the previous one.

"Would you like to take a shower?"

"A shower sounds wonderful," he murmured, rolling his shoulders to work out the kinks in his muscles. A hot shower would feel great. "Just give me a minute to enjoy this."

With a giggle, she snuggled into him, letting him hold her in the crook of his arm. The rush of power that came from having her beneath him and acknowledged as her Master, was slowly diminishing to a more normal level, leaving him feeling a little empty yet very satisfied.

After a few minutes of cuddling, they moved to the shower, where he had the pleasure of washing her hair, then soaping her all over. There was nothing sexual about it, but being able to wash her was an element of aftercare he'd missed when they'd been playing mostly at the club, especially since she'd rarely stayed to shower when they'd played at his place.

Leaving kisses across her skin as he cleaned her, he grinned when she returned the favor—giving extra special attention to cleaning his dick. Two rounds of bubbles were necessary before she gave the tip a little kiss.

Curled around her in her bed, her damp hair tickling his face, Gavin felt as though he was where he was meant to be—where he wanted to be for the rest of his life.

Tightening his arms around her, he buried his face in the back of her neck.

"I love you, *mo chridhe.*"

Soft fingers stroked down his arm as her whisper came back through the darkness.

"I love you, too, Master."

EPILOGUE

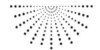

GAVIN

He couldn't breathe. He tried to inhale, but all he got was... fluff?

A squalling, outraged shriek filled his ears when he pushed the thing off his face.

"Oliver!" Leah's elbow jabbed into Gavin's side as she sat up beside him. When he opened his eyes, the orange fluffball was firmly lodged in Leah's arms, purring up a storm. "Oh, I'm sorry, baby. Did Gavin scare you?"

"Considering he just tried to murder me, I'm pretty sure I'm the one who should be scared," Gavin muttered, falling back on the pillow. This wasn't how he'd expected to wake up this morning, but since he was in bed next to a naked Leah, it wasn't all bad.

"Was he on your face?" Strangely Leah sounded delighted.

"Yeah. How did he even get in here?" They'd closed the door last night when they'd come into the bedroom to keep him out, which hadn't seemed to bother him at the time.

"He must have come in when I got up to use the bathroom. This means he likes you. I often wake up with him cuddled up to my head and sometimes on my face. Aw, you don't know any better, do you, Oliver?"

If that was 'liking' him, Gavin could have done without it, but he had to admit the kitten was a cute little bugger when it crawled out of Leah's arms and came to lie on the center of his chest. The vibrations of its purrs rumbled through him.

"See? He likes you."

And that made Leah happy.

Sighing inwardly, Gavin stroked the little kitten's back and was rewarded with little claws kneading his chest. They were fairly blunt, thankfully, and so more uncomfortable than painful.

"Look at you, making muffins." Leah nuzzled the top of Oliver's head with her nose, then moved upward to give Gavin a kiss.

Okay, he supposed he could get used to this.

"What do you want for breakfast?"

"Well, I was hoping to have you, but there's a cat on my chest." Not exactly the kind of morning pussy he'd been anticipating. "Am I allowed to move when there's a cat on me?"

Laughing, Leah leaned over to give him another kiss. This time, Gavin caught her by the back of her neck, holding her in position.

With a sound of disgust, Oliver got to his feet and stalked away, allowing Gavin to move freely again.

In the now kitten-free bed, Gavin gave Leah a proper good morning fucking that made her late to work—not that she seemed to mind.

LEAH

Having Gavin over to her house wasn't a magical fix to everything, of course, but she had to admit that within a week, it made a difference. She felt happier, more open, more willing to be vulnerable, and less afraid she would be hurt.

If nothing else, knowing how dedicated he was to make things work this time, even doing things he was uncomfortable with, made all the difference.

For someone who had never been interested in having a cat, he'd started spoiling *hers* terribly, and Oliver couldn't get enough of him. They were pretty cute together. Oliver was growing at a fast rate, but he still looked tiny when he was perched on Gavin's knee—and sometimes his shoulder when Gavin was sitting on the couch. Seeing them together made her flush with happiness.

It didn't entirely get rid of the little niggle of anxiety in her stomach things wouldn't work out—and now she'd be left with a heartbroken cat along with her own heartbreak—but she had hope. She could look at her worries with a more critical eye and file them firmly under 'currently baseless.'

She wished she could do the same for her friends.

Wednesday game night was a little awkward, what with Gavin and Leah's knowledge of Jax's lies. Aiden and Cyana were clueless but astute enough to realize something was going on. Thankfully, neither of them was the type to speak up without knowing more.

Jax seemed confused, and Esther was... well, she was putting on a good show of being herself, but those who were closest to her could tell something was off.

At least the campaign was going well. Their fictional dog was now armored, well-fed, and happily traveling with them, much to Gavin's clear dismay. It cracked Leah up how annoyed he was at their investment in the fictional dog. He should have known better than to create that chart, so they knew who the dog liked the best.

Esther and Jax had been the last to arrive, and they were the first to leave without anyone getting a chance to separate for extra chitchatting. Leah suspected Esther didn't want to talk about it, and she knew she would have to if she left Jax's side, especially with Cyana's curiosity roused. Since Esther was keeping it to herself, Leah couldn't tell Cyana either, so her nerves ticked up when Cyana pulled her to the side before she left.

Thankfully, Cyana didn't want to talk about Esther and Jax. She wanted to talk about Gavin and Leah.

"You seem happier." Cyana studied her face closely. "If he messes up again, I'll kick his ass."

"It wasn't just him," Leah said defensively. Yeah, there had been a lot of things he'd done wrong, from her perspective, but she'd been guilty of the lack of communication that had led to the deterioration of their marriage the first time around. "And he's trying."

Cyana smiled approvingly. "Good to hear it. Want to tell me what's going on with Jax and Esther?"

Dammit. She'd known that was coming.

"I don't know everything, and what I do know, I can't tell."

"Understood." Cyana's gaze was thoughtful. "Hopefully, Esther will feel up to telling me soon." Probably sooner rather than later now that Cyana had noticed. Leah had the feeling Esther was still trying to decide what she wanted to do and wanted to be prepared with that before telling Cyana what was going on. As hard as it was for Leah to be patient while Esther figured things out, it would be even harder for Cyana, their Momma Bear friend.

Cyana went out the door with Aiden, who insisted on walking her to her car under the pretense of trying to get in her pants. They bounced insults off each other the whole way.

Grinning, Leah watched them go. Her smiled widened when Gavin came up behind her, wrapping his arms around her waist.

"How are you doing?" he asked, nuzzling the back of her neck. "Everything okay with Cyana?"

"Yeah. She was curious about Esther and Jax."

Gavin blew out a long sigh, loosening his hold, so she could turn around and look at him.

"Do you think we should tell Jax?" The question made her anxious because she didn't have an answer, but it also made her smile at him, glad he was asking her opinion.

"I don't know." He'd seemed to realize something was going on with Esther but clearly didn't know what. Both of them had been pretending everything was okay, which meant everyone else followed their lead. For now. "Esther specifically asked for time to think about what she was going to do."

"Then we'll give her time." Gavin's gaze traveled over her face, his blue eyes introspective. "Eventually, if she doesn't talk to Jax, I'd like to revisit the topic. Especially if things stay as tense between them as they were tonight."

Jax was his friend, and he didn't want to see his friend suffering. Leah got it. On the other hand, she wasn't against seeing Jax going through some of the same confusion and doubts that had plagued Esther for months now. It wouldn't do Jax any harm to stew a little. They wouldn't be able to let the situation go on for too long without intervening.

"I'll want to talk to Esther before you do that," she said, feeling a little guilty since that was what Gavin had requested for Jax. At the very least, she owed her friend a head's up, what Gavin had wanted to give Jax.

Gavin smiled, pulling her in for a reassuring kiss, and she relaxed. His lips left hers, and he tucked her head under his chin, holding her against him and letting her lean on him.

"We'll figure it out together."

That sounded good.

"Are we talking to Mitch tomorrow?" They'd agreed they wanted to let their son know what was going on—another way they were making things official between them.

Long ago, she'd thought the wedding was the big ending, the big happily-ever-after moment, and after that, everything would ride along smoothly, but that wasn't how life or relationships worked. Happily-ever-after was a choice, a promise, and it took both people and working on it every day.

She believed she and Gavin were going to make it happen this time around.

"Absolutely." Gavin kissed her thoroughly, setting her nerves humming, before pulling away. "I need to tell him I hope to ask his mum to marry me again by the end of this year."

Laughing, it was Leah's turn to pull him back down for a kiss.

She already knew she was going to say yes.

ESTHER

Thursday night, Jax texted to say he had to work late. Of course. He'd been working late every Thursday night for months now. Something she hadn't told her friends because she hadn't wanted to acknowledge the truth.

Something she'd read in every advice column about being married to a cheater.

I ignored the signs because I didn't want to know.

Tears pricked her eyes, and she bit down on her lower lip. It had been a lot easier before Leah had told her Jax hadn't been with Gavin and Aiden at the gym on Sundays. Now that she knew he was lying, it was impossible to ignore the unhappiness churning in her gut and the certainty she was losing her husband.

If she was in the stages of grief, she was pretty sure she hadn't made it past the first stage yet.

Shock and denial.

There was still a part of her that wanted to believe in Jax, wanted to believe in them as a couple, wanted to believe there was some other reason he'd been so busy lately with so many late nights, some other reason he was lying about his whereabouts on Sunday afternoons.

A few days ago, she'd done the unthinkable and felt guilty. She'd gone through his phone. There hadn't been anything suspicious, so she'd done something even worse—she'd downloaded an app that would allow her to use *her* phone to track *his* phone. Now, she kept bringing it up to see where he was when he was working late.

Before dinner, he'd still been at the university.

Now that dinner was over, and she'd sent Jennifer and Daniel off to their rooms to finish up their homework, she brought up her side of the app again. Unhappy anxiety swirled in her stomach, and she tasted bile in the back of her throat as if everything she'd just eaten was going to come back up again.

I have to know.

She had to know, then decide what she was going to do.

Something she'd been putting off for days.

Jax knew something was up, but he was working late tonight, anyway. She wasn't great at hiding when something was bothering her. She wanted to believe he really was working, that he wouldn't have gone to do... whatever it was he was doing, knowing there was something off with her.

When she pulled up the phone app, it was immediately obvious he wasn't at the university. He was in a residential neighborhood, and her stomach dropped.

Thirty minutes of internet stalking later, she was staring at the Facebook photo of a gorgeous blonde, poised and put-together, who worked at the university and lived at the house Jax's phone was currently still sitting in.

Shock and denial.

The latter was no longer an option, but the former was in full effect.

What did she do now?

******

What is Jax up to? Has Esther been married the wrong man all these years? Or will they get a second chance of happiness as well? CLICK HERE to download Dungeon Daddy and find out!

Or, if you wanted to know more about Mitch, Gavin and Leah's son, CLICK HERE to read his story in the first Masters of Marquis book, Bondage Buddies!

ABOUT THE AUTHOR

Golden Angel is a USA Today best-selling author and self-described bibliophile with a "kinky" bent who loves to write stories for the characters in her head. If she didn't get them out, she's pretty sure she'd go just a little crazy.

She is happily married, old enough to know better but still too young to care, and a big fan of happily-ever-afters, strong heroes and heroines, and sizzling chemistry.

When she's not writing, she can often be found on the couch reading, in front of her sewing machine making a new cosplay, hanging out with her friends, or wandering the Maryland Renaissance Fair.

www.goldenangelromance.com

BB bookbub.com/authors/golden-angel
g goodreads.com/goldeniangel
f facebook.com/GoldenAngelAuthor
○ instagram.com/goldeniangel

OTHER BOOKS BY GOLDEN ANGEL

CONTEMPORARY BDSM ROMANCE

Venus Rising Series (MFM Romance)

The Venus School

Venus Aspiring

Venus Desiring

Venus Transcendent

Venus Wedding

Venus Rising Box Set

Stronghold Doms Series

The Sassy Submissive

Taming the Tease

Mastering Lexie

Pieces of Stronghold

Breaking the Chain

Bound to the Past

Stripping the Sub

Tempting the Domme

Hardcore Vanilla

Steamy Stocking Stuffers

Entering Stronghold Box Set

Nights at Stronghold Box Set

Stronghold: Closing Time Box Set

Masters of Marquis Series

Bondage Buddies

Master Chef

Law & Disorder

Dungeons & Doms Series

Dungeon Master

Dungeon Daddy

Dungeon Showdown

Poker Loser Trilogy

Forced Bet

Back in the Game

Winning Hand

Poker Loser Trilogy Bundle (3 books in 1!)

Standalones - Daddy Doms

Chef Daddy

Little Villain

HISTORICAL SPANKING ROMANCE

Domestic Discipline Quartet

Birching His Bride

Dealing With Discipline

Punishing His Ward

Claiming His Wife

The Domestic Discipline Quartet Box Set

Bridal Discipline Series

Philip's Rules

Gabrielle's Discipline

Lydia's Penance

Benedict's Commands

Arabella's Taming

Pride and Punishment Box Set

Commands and Consequences Box Set

Deception and Discipline

A Season for Treason

A Season for Scandal

A Season for Smugglers

A Season for Spies

Bridgewater Brides

Their Harlot Bride

Standalone

Marriage Training

Rogue Booty

SCI-FI ROMANCE

Tsenturion Masters Series with Lee Savino

Alien Captive

Alien Tribute

Alien Abduction

Standalone

Mated on Hades

SHIFTER ROMANCE

Big Bad Bunnies Series

Chasing His Bunny

Chasing His Squirrel

Chasing His Puma

Chasing His Polar Bear

Chasing His Honey Badger

Chasing Her Lion

Night of the Wild Stags

Chasing Tail Box Set

Chasing Tail... Again Box Set

Printed in Great Britain
by Amazon